To
Julie

Father of The Bride

Edward Streeter

Edward

Large Print

THORNDIKE PRESS • THORNDIKE, MAINE

1948, 1949   202p

LC: 83-18025

Library of Congress Cataloging in Publication Data:

Streeter, Edward, 1891-
   Father of the bride.

       (Print)
   1. Large type books. I. Title.
[PS3537.T828F3   1984]   813'.52   83-18025
ISBN 0-89621-500-8

Large Print edition available through arrangement with Simon
& Schuster, Inc.

Cover design by Andy Winther.

Contents

Chapter 1

THE GREAT DECISION

No matter what Kay might have done about marriage it would not have been looked upon with any great favor by Mr. Stanley Banks, merely because he happened to be fonder of his first-born than he realized.

During her teens he had dismissed all aspirants with a contemptuous snort. From the time that Kay had first revealed herself to the social world, minus a mouthful of braces and plus a permanent, leggy adolescents with porcupine hair had begun to beat a path to 24 Maple Drive. Mr. Banks had regarded these inarticulate sufferers with a jaundiced eye.

If they caused him any uneasiness it had been wasted. Not that Kay spurned male attention, but, during those exciting days, she preferred it to be universal rather than specific. Nature had endowed her with what amounted to a season pass to every dance, sporting event and week-end party that her strength permitted

– and she had the stamina of a six-day bicycle rider.

She was also restrained by an early infatuation for her English teacher, a brilliant young man with large front teeth and a tendency to stomach ulcers, who had once told her that she had an intellect. This otherwise unconfirmed diagnosis gave her secret ambitions. The result was that the youths who fluttered around her with such unco-ordinated eagerness seemed callow to her beautiful blue eyes. Lord Byron and Leonardo da Vinci being dead, the field had struck her as limited.

And so the tender years had slipped by. With their passing Mr. Banks' emotional pendulum had swung the other way. He found himself wondering what was wrong with the child. What was it that caused men to bob into her life for a few brief weeks or months – and then disappear forever? She couldn't go on being a bridesmaid until she was an old lady!

It worried him and unconsciously his attitude changed, even toward Kay's most casual acquaintances. Unlike the old days, when he had been curt, suspicious and, on occasions, frankly hostile, he now began to receive them with an open-armed cordiality that would have driven any alert young male out into a snowstorm.

Then suddenly — without warning — it was obvious that something was happening to Kay. Some alchemy was at work within her. There was a light in her eyes that none of Dr. Barnes' vitamins had ever kindled. The fashionable, dead-pan expression that she usually wore for home use was replaced with a radiance that made her, at times, almost a stranger to Mr. Banks.

"What's gotten into Kay, Ellie? She acts queer to me."

"I don't know," said Mrs. Banks. "Maybe she's in love."

Mr. Banks made noises of contempt. "In love! Who would she be in love with?"

"I haven't the wildest idea."

"Nonsense," said Mr. Banks. "You must have some idea."

"Well, do you remember that about two weeks ago Kay said she'd met a boy named Buckley Something-or-other at a cocktail party?"

"Never heard of him," said Mr. Banks.

"Of course you have, dear. Don't *try* to be stupid. And do you remember that a few nights later he came here to take her to some cocktail party?"

"You don't mean that big overgrown ham with the shoulders? Listen, Ellie, you women

11

jump at the damnedest conclusions. Just because a man —"

"All right. I'm wrong. You just wait and see."

They waited, and as the days passed it became apparent that Buckley was coming more sharply into focus. His name crept into Kay's chatter with increasing frequency, though always casually. It had never been very clear to Mr. Banks just where Kay spent her time, but wherever it was Buckley evidently spent his there also. Furthermore, he was apparently a young man with decided views on everything from football to God — views which, for Kay's money, had not been equaled since the Delphic oracles went out of business.

Mr. Banks felt a resurgence of his old attitude. This new moth, which was beginning to fly so close to the flame, became definitely distasteful to him.

"I don't think much of that fellow," he said to Mrs. Banks after Buckley had spent a painful ten minutes in the living room waiting for Kay.

"I don't know, dear," said Mrs. Banks. "Why don't you just leave Kay alone and let her work things out for herself?"

"I'm not interfering with her," said Mr. Banks crossly. "You're the one that's always worrying."

A hush of anticipation had fallen over the Banks family as in a theater just before the curtain rises — but nothing happened. Kay continued to look dreamy. Buckley, during his brief appearances, maintained his air of uneasy aloofness. After a few stiff moments they would both rush, unleashed, into the night.

Then, unexpectedly, the storm broke.

They were gathered round the dinner table on one of the increasingly rare occasions when Kay ate at home.

"Where are the boys?" asked Mr. Banks.

"They've gone to a night game with Joe Stanley," said Mrs. Banks. "They couldn't wait for dinner. Ben said they'd pick up something to eat in town."

"Don't those two boys ever stay at home for a meal?" grumbled Mr. Banks.

Kay sighed. "Ben's not a *boy*, Pops. He's a man. He's old enough to have a family."

"Well, Tommy isn't," said Mr. Banks. "He's in high school and he's supposed to stay home nights and do some work."

"Oh, by the way, Mom, that reminds me. I won't be home this week end," said Kay.

"Where are you going, dear?" asked Mrs. Banks.

"I'm going to spend it with Buckley's family."

13

Mr. Banks dropped an unbroken cracker into his soup. "Look here," he asked, "are you going to marry this character?"

"I guess so," replied Kay. She continued to work on her soup. Her tone had been so even and casual that the import of her words did not immediately register, and the conversation threatened to end on this simple note. As a matter of fact it did for quite a while. Nothing could be heard but the thoughtful intake of cream of tomato.

Mrs. Banks broke the silence. "And when," she asked with timid sarcasm, "are you thinking of getting married?"

"I really don't know, Mother. It all depends on Buckley's *plans.*" Kay's voice was that of a tired kindergarten teacher. "It might be months or it might be in a few weeks — or it might be just any time at *all.* We can't *tell* yet. And there's one thing — we *won't* be pinned down. Buckley's *very* decided about that sort of thing. He just *won't* be pinned down."

Mr. Banks felt his neck begin to push against his collar. He took a long drink of water. "I hope," he said in a strained voice, "that Buckley won't think I'm nosy or trying to pin him down if I ask a few simple questions."

Kay looked bored. "O.K., Pops. I suppose

14

we have to go *through* this. It does seem to me, though —"

"Well, to begin with, who the hell is this Buckley anyway?"

"Now, Pops, please. If we're going —"

"— and what's his last name? I hope its better than his first one."

"Pops, I'm not going to sit here —"

"— and where the hell does he come from — and who does he think is going to support him? If it's me he's got another guess coming. And who in God's name —"

Mrs. Banks interrupted. "Stanley, nobody's deaf and you don't have to swear every other word. It's just plain mortifying with Delilah in the kitchen listening. You don't give Kay a chance. Let her —"

At that moment Kay, the darling of his heart, turned on him for the first time in her life. "Listen, Pops, I'm twenty-four years old and Buckley's twenty-six and we're grown *people* — and as far as your supporting *Buckley*, I'll tell you right now he's the kind that wouldn't let *anybody* support him. He'd rather *die* first.

"*That's* the kind of person he is. He's a *wonderful* person. He's the kind of person that's absolutely — I mean *absolutely* — independent. The kind that will always take care of his own.

15

You don't need to worry about *that*, Pops – *ever*. Buckley wouldn't come to you for help not even if we were starving in the *gutter*.

"And his name is *Dunstan. That's* what it is – Buckley Dunstan. And he's a *wonderful* businessman – I mean a *really* wonderful businessman – and – and he has a wonderful *job.*"

"Doing what?" asked Mr. Banks, seizing the first factual straw.

"Oh, I don't *know*, Pops. He makes something. Does it *really* make any difference what it is? He's the kind of person that can do *anything* – anything at all.

"As for his *parents* – well, I'll tell you this, Pops – they're just as good as you and *Mom.*" There was a suggestion in her voice that this was an understatement. "They're *swell* people and they live in East Smithfield and I guess you'll agree that East Smithfield is just as good a place as Fairview *Manor* – although I don't see what that's got to do with it *anyway.*"

Mr. Banks agreed silently.

His blood pressure had gone down as quickly as it had risen. He scarcely heard what Kay was saying and he had forgotten all about Buckley. He was looking at his daughter's flushed face and remembering a small girl with brown pigtails and dirty overalls who used to fly at her two younger brothers when they

16

goaded her too far.

It seemed like such an incredibly short time ago. That was all. He had a panicky feeling that tears were coming into his eyes. Rising from his chair, he kissed the top of her head.

"O.K., Kitten," he said. "I love him already. What did you say his last name was?"

At this point Mr. Banks began to come down with some strange kind of psychic rash. From the night of that conversation at the dinner table he could feel it creeping through his system. With a detachment which was anything but calm, he watched himself change from a logical, well-balanced lawyer into an unreasoning, anxiety-ridden psychopathic. It disturbed him so that he did not even mention it to Mrs. Banks.

Each night he lay on his back in the darkness, his hands folded across his chest like a figure on a sarcophagus in Westminster Abbey. A street lamp threw a milky patch of light on a corner of the bedroom ceiling. The intervening foliage of a tree caused it to shimmer like water. He stared at it rigidly, struggling to make his mind a blank.

Who was this bounder who had invaded the sanctity of his home and snatched his child from under his nose? Child — that's what she

17

was — a child. What did she know about the qualities in a man which are so necessary to a successful marriage? She was only a child who, a few months ago, was running around in pigtails — was it a few months or a few years?

He mustn't let himself go on like this or he would be a gibbering idiot in the office tomorrow.

Snatched. That was the word for it. She was sleeping in her own room, but only in body. Her spirit had moved out. She would always love them of course, but never in the old way — never again with her whole trusting, needing self. From here in her love would be doled out like a farmer's wife tossing scraps to the family rooster.

What mawkish bunk! He *must* cut it out. Wasn't this what he'd always been building up to? He flopped over on his side and tried burying his face in the crook of his arm. He had sometimes found self-smothering helpful.

He knew that, under similar circumstances, he wouldn't feel this way about Ben and Tommy. Somehow or other Kay was more indentified with those early years of married life than either of the boys. He had been used to the idea of parenthood by the time they arrived. Kay had been born in the uncertain days when his relationship to the firm of

18

Barthlum, Henderson and Peck had been as nebulous as his salary – years before he had been made a junior partner and they had bought the white shingled house in Fairview Manor. It had been a happy period in spite of the struggle – a period unmarred by the adolescent features of any questing male.

Well, the beans were spilt now! Casually! Over a cup of tomato soup! Not asking by your leave, but giving him the devil for trying to find out what the goon's last name was! Outside of his name, what else did Kay know about him? Oh, yes. He was wonderful. That was going to be a great help when he started to raise a family.

Could he support a family? That was the point. How could he know that this guy had what it took? Up to date he'd sounded vaguer than dishwater every time he'd opened his mouth. An impractical dreamer –that's what he was. Kay was an idealist and she'd fallen for this fellow because he agreed with all her ideas and didn't make any sense.

He flopped onto his other side and looked over at Mrs. Banks. She seemed to be sleeping peacefully. Women were inconsistent creatures. If the kids were out at some little dance she couldn't sleep until she heard them come in. But when it was a question of how (or if) her only daughter was going to eat for the rest of her life, she fell asleep like a baby.

Wise men never discuss topics of a potentially upsetting nature until they have finished their breakfast. The wisest refuse to talk at all until they have been spiritually fortified by a couple of fried eggs.

For many years this had been one of Mr. Banks' ground rules. It was a sound, functional rule, for by the time he had gulped his breakfast he was invariably late for the eight-fifteen. One could not get into much of a controversy while trotting from the breakfast table to the garage. Thus the day was automatically started right and morning problems, like morning mists, had a tendency to disperse as the sun rose higher.

But Mr. Banks was no longer a wise man. During these last few days (and nights) he had become aware that his sense of balance was being dragged from under him like sand under the impact of surf.

To his surprise Mrs. Banks did not seem to share his apprehensions although she was usually the timid one when faced with change. On the contrary, she seemed to float through her days in a state of ecstasy. This was an added annoyance to Mr. Banks.

From her casual remarks it become gradually clear to him that her mind was not on Buckley at all, but rather on the ceremony which he promised to bring into being and on the material things connected with it — on dresses and hats and shoes — on underwear and sheets and towels — on all the thousand things which, to a woman, truly legalize a marriage.

He had always known that, at heart, Mrs. Banks was a natural-born purchasing agent, although her talents had been somewhat restricted by circumstances. Now at last she was presented with a buyers' field day, fully authorized and aboveboard, and she was merely letting her imagination take a trial run around the track to get the stiffness out of its joints.

Mr. Banks was standing before the medicine cabinet mirror, thoughtfully lathering his face. It rather pleased him to think that he could detect lines in it that had not been there a week before.

"Kay's going to make a beautiful bride," murmured Mrs. Banks dreamily, half to herself, half to Mr. Banks' pajamaed back. "She's got just the figure and the coloring. I know exactly the kind of dress she should have — the sleeves long and tight-fitting — and the skirt —"

Mr. Banks' hand trembled and a drop of blood discolored the soap on his chin. The stout, dependable dam which had heretofore restrained his morning thoughts gave way without warning. Over Mrs. Banks' unprepared head poured the swollen torrent of his accumulated apprehensions.

He was possessed of a doomsday eloquence. As he warmed up to his theme it began to sound like a description of Hiroshima. She listened in dismay to the recital of possibilities that she had not even considered. By the time her husband's emotional reservoir was emptied he had missed three trains to the city. Shaken to the roots, she did not attempt to follow him downstairs.

When she heard him slam up the patent garage door she watched anxiously from the bedroom window as he backed the sedan into the drive and disappeared around the corner in a spray of gravel.

Mr. Banks found himself a seat on the eight-forty-two and opened his morning paper. Theoretically his day was ruined. Actually, and to his surprise, he was conscious of a pleasant feeling of lightness. The sun shone impartially on the alternating garbage dumps and suburban developments that flashed past the window. The air was dry and bracing. The world was suddenly beginning to snap back into place.

His pleasure at this discovery was dimmed at the edges, however, by a small gnawing sense of guilt lest he might have upset Ellie unduly. Women were so emotional about these matters and inclined to take them overseriously. He toyed with the idea of calling her up when he got to town. Then he became interested in the paper and forgot about it.

But not so Mrs. Banks. All day long the Seidlitz powder of anxiety which her husband had dumped into her tranquil soul seethed and boiled within her. As she made her rounds from the A. & P. Supermarket to Kohoe's Fish Store to Sammy Lee's Hand Laundry, the uneasiness within her mounted to a bubbling panic.

She was not a complex person. Although she had strong instinctive convictions, years of battering by the massed forces of male reasoning caused moments when her self-confidence wavered.

Of course she never let Mr. Banks know about these weaknesses. Under attack she would defend her position as if it were the Alamo. But in this particular case she had had no chance to fight. The onslaught had been so unexpected and violent that it had left her stunned. Until this moment her world had seemed so beautiful. Now it lay in pieces about her.

When Mr. Banks re-entered the house that evening he still retained the pleasant sensation of being at once relaxed and gathered and he hummed a little tune as he threw his hat on the shelf on the coat closet. Mrs. Banks came out of the living room and put her hands on his shoulders. As he kissed her he was surprised by the worried look in her eyes. One might have thought she had been crying.

"Stan, I'm so upset about Kay."

"Kay? What's the matter with Kay? What's she done now?" he asked absent-mindedly, removing his overcoat.

"Oh, Stan, suppose Buckley *shouldn't* be the man for her. How can *we* tell? We know so little about him. And she's *so* young. Suppose he *didn't* have business judgment and *couldn't* earn a decent living. Suppose he made Kay *unhappy*. Suppose —"

Mr. Banks stopped fumbling for the coathook. He stared at her in amazement. "For heaven's sake, Ellie, what in the world's getting into you? For years you've been worried about Kay's not getting married. Now she finds herself a perfectly nice guy and you get the jitters. I'll bet he'll do a better job than that poopadoop you were so crazy about that hung around here all last winter."

He took her chin in his cupped hand and gazed down at her thoughtfully. "You know what, darling? I think you're tired. You've been going it too hard lately. You've got to take care of yourself. Tell you what I'll do. I'll knock together a couple of old-fashioneds. It'll do you good. And we'll drink a little toast to the bride and groom."

Chapter 2

GETTING
ACQUAINTED

Buckley, Kay informed her parents with her best Old School irony, *also* had a father and mother. It seemed to her that the situation called for a minimum display of interest from the Banks family unless, of course, they preferred to make it look like a shot-gun wedding and introduce themselves at the altar rail.

Mr. Banks agreed moodily. The obvious fact that he must do something about meeting Buckley's family had been weighing on him for some time. Although he had never considered himself a shy man, the idea gave him as much pleasure as a summons to appear before a congressional committee. He had been postponing action from day to day in the same way that he put off wearing a pair of new shoes to the office.

"I suppose Kay's right," he admitted gloomily to Mrs. Banks. "We've got to face it."

"I don't understand why you get in such a lather about it," she said. "What's so awful about meeting Buckley's father and mother?"

"Who said I was in a lather?" he retorted sharply. "All I mean is you'd think Kay might have picked out somebody we knew instead of a family we never laid eyes on and that are probably God-awful. I just know the kind of people they are. It's going to be terrible."

"Stanley Banks, for a grown man you sometimes don't make any sense. In the first place I don't see why you assume the Dunstans are terrible and in the second you're not marrying Buckley's family."

"I might just as well be," groaned Mr. Banks. "I'll probably have to support them."

The Dunstans eventually took matters into their own hands and invited Mr. and Mrs. Banks to East Smithfield for Sunday dinner; just the four of them – without Kay and Buckley – so they could get acquainted.

"That's the pay-off," said Mr. Banks. "They're the cozy type."

He made no further comment, but during the intervening days he showed all the symptoms of a debutante about to be introduced at Buckingham Palace. On Sunday morning he dressed carefully in a sport coat

27

and slacks, then went upstairs after breakfast and changed into a business suit. He insisted on starting half an hour earlier than was necessary – just to allow for a blowout or something. The result was that they arrived in East Smithfield shortly after twelve.

Mr. Banks said he'd be damned if he was going to sit and moon at the Dunstans' for an hour. He preferred to slum around the town and get a line on the natives.

"I'll bet they won't even have a drink before dinner," he said gloomily.

"How do you know they won't?"

"Because I know. That's the kind of people they are."

"Well, suppose they don't. You're not an alcoholic, are you?"

Mr. Banks sighed but didn't pursue the argument.

"I think it might be more intelligent to find out where the Dunstans live instead of driving around aimlessly," said Mrs. Banks. "At least we won't end up by being late."

"I'll bet it's a shack," said Mr. Banks.

When they finally located it, the Dunstan shack turned out to be a large, whitewashed brick house about a mile out of town. It sat well back from the road surrounded by old elm trees. The discovery that it was at least twice the size of his own seemed to add fuel to Mr. Banks' agitation. He looked at his watch.

"I'm going back to that hotel we passed and wash up," he announced.

"Nonsense," said Mrs. Banks. "You can wash at the Dunstans'. They probably have running water."

"I prefer to wash at the hotel," said Mr. Banks with dignity. She sensed that this was not the time to cross him.

When they drew up in front of the hotel he did not suggest that she get out, but hurried through the revolving doors. On his return, ten mintues later, it was obvious that he was more composed. The interior of the sedan immediately took on the Saturday night odor of a bar-and-grill.

"Stanley Banks, you've been drinking."

Mr. Banks did not take his eyes off the road ahead. "Why is it," he asked, "that a person can't take a casual drink without being accused of 'drinking'? It does seem to me that a man over fifty —"

"I think it's perfectly outrageous for you to meet the Dunstans smelling like an old whiskey bottle. It's humiliating, that's what it is. What in the world's gotten into you? And Sunday morning, too."

"What's Sunday morning got to do with it?"

29

asked Mr. Banks, hoping to divert the argument. But Mrs. Banks was still being difficult when they turned in at the Dunstans' entrance.

The first meeting of the in-laws is comparable to the original hookup of the Lewis and Clark Expedition with the Rocky Mountain Indians.

In the latter instance it is recorded that for a brief moment after the encounter both sides glared at one another with mingled hostility and curiosity. At this point a false move would have been fatal. If anyone had so much as reached for his tobacco pouch the famous Journals would never have seen the light of day.

Then, each side finding the other apparently unarmed, the tension eased. The leaders stepped forward, embraced, rubbed noses and muttered "How." Skins were spread and refreshments laid on them by squaws. The party was in the bag.

The Banks-Dunstan meeting followed similar lines. For a split second the two families stared at one another in the Dunstan entrance hall. During that instant Mrs. Banks took inventory of Mrs. Dunstan from hair-do to shoes. Mrs. Dunstan did the same for Mrs. Banks. Then, finding everything mutually satisfactory, they approached one another with out-stretched arms, embraced and said, "My dear."

The two males merely shook hands awkwardly and said in unison, "It certainly is nice to meet you."

Mrs. Dunstan started to lead the way into the living room. "Would you like to wash your hands?" asked Mr. Dunstan.

"I've washed them," said Mr. Banks, glancing at him suspiciously.

"I can't tell you how crazy we are about your Kay," said Mrs. Dunstan.

"Well, that's just the way we feel about Buckley," said Mrs. Banks.

"Yes indeed," said Mr. Banks. Obviously something was called for.

As far as he was concerned that seemed about all there was to be said. He would have been quite ready to second a motion to adjourn.

The situation was saved by the appearance of a maid with a shaker full of martinis and a tray of hot hors d'oeuvres. Mr. Banks looked at this arrangement with pleased incredulity.

He took a martini and found it excellent. "I think we should drink to the bride and groom," said Mr. Dunstan. Mr. Banks drank deeply and relaxed like a deflating balloon. Mr. Dunstan refilled the glasses.

Warmed by this unexpected hospitality and

31

his previous wash-up at the hotel, Mr. Banks felt impelled to words. "This is an important occasion," he said. "My wife and I have been looking forward to it for a long time. Personally I thought your son was a great fellow the moment I set eyes on him. Now that I've met his father and mother I like him even better. From here in I forsee that the Dunstan-Banks families will beat as one."

"I am sure we're going to be most congenial," said Mrs. Dunstan apprehensively, "and do call us Doris and Herbert, not Mr. and Mrs. Dunstan."

"And Stanley and Ellie," said Mrs. Banks somewhat overeagerly.

There was an embarrassed silence.

"Have you ever been in Fairview Manor, Herbert?" asked Mr. Banks.

"No, we haven't, Stanley. We've heard a lot about it, of course."

"I love your house, Doris," said Mrs. Banks, who had by this time sized up and appraised critically every article of furniture in the living room.

"Thank you, Ellie. We like it. I'm crazy to see yours. Buckley's always talking about it."

"Another, Stan?" asked Mr. Dunstan.

"Well, just to help you out, Herb," said Mr. Banks.

His wife moved over beside him. "You'd better watch your step," she muttered.

It was too late. The release from supertension was more than he could combat. He graciously helped his friend Herb finish up the shaker.

"I think dinner is ready," said Mrs. Dunstan, who had known it for a long time.

She led the way toward the dining room. "You've got a wonderful place here, Edith," said Mrs. Banks, falling in beside her.

"Doris," she said. "Won't you sit there, Ellie. And now we want to hear all about our new daughter."

"I'm afraid there isn't much to tell," said Mrs. Banks.

"Nonsense," said Mr. Banks. "Would you like to hear the story about how Ellie left Kay in her baby carriage outside the A. & P. and then forgot about her and went home?"

He told them in hilarious detail. A flood of memories and anecdotes poured from him like a mountain brook. He took them through Kay's childhood and school days step by step. Then, as a kind of appendix, he gave them a detailed account of his own boyhood, early manhood and married life. Occasionally one of the Dunstans broke in with a comment. Toward the end of the meal they ceased to compete.

33

After dinner Mr. Banks picked out a comfortable-looking chair in the darkest corner of the living room. He felt suddenly drowsy. "Now," he said, "you must tell us all about Buckley." The desire to take just forty winks became overpowering. As Buckley entered his first year in high school Mr. Banks' eyes closed and he was instantly asleep.

They drove back to Fairview Manor late in the afternoon, Mrs. Banks at the controls. Mr. Banks felt relaxed and happy. It was hard for him to understand why he had dreaded this meeting so much. He sought in vain among his acquaintances for a finer family than the Dunstans. Certainly no one could have been easier to talk to. He hummed a contented little song. Mrs. Banks said nothing.

Chapter 3

FINANCIAL MATTERS

It was quite clear to Mr. Banks that things couldn't drift along like this forever. When two people decided to get married they announced their engagement and then there was a wedding. The only question was when.

As his mind focused on the actual ceremony he began to have secret qualms about it. Weddings had never meant much to him one way or the other. They were pleasant parties where he was apt to run into a lot of people whom he had not seen lately. Now, when he considered his role as father of the bride, it became alarmingly apparent that he was slated to play a lead part in what looked more and more to him like a public spectacle. Unconsciously he was experiencing the first symptoms of aisle-shyness.

When it came to discussing the date, therefore, he was like a man who has rashly committed himself to go swimming in a glacial stream. His idea was either to get the affair over as quickly as possible or else postpone it to a point so far distant in time that, like death, he wouldn't have to worry about it for the present at least.

Mrs. Banks, on the other hand, looked at the matter more from the point of view of a stage manager. How long would it take to prepare the costumes, build the scenery and collect the props? She concluded that, working day and night, the production might be staged in three months — not a minute earlier.

During the discussions that followed Buckley remained unusually silent. He was obviously a young man who was not used to getting married and these unfolding and complex plans seemed to bewilder him. As he listened to his future mother-in-law he became gradually panic-stricken. He explained to her with desperate finality that he was a simple fellow who wanted no trappings or lugs. His idea of a wedding was a little ivy-covered chapel in some lovely country spot where he and Kay could walk down the aisle hand in hand.

Mr. Banks decided to switch the conversation into lighter vein. Buckley was inclined to have a heavy touch at moments. He said that was a fine idea. He liked it. The trouble was that the only kind of ivy that grew around Fairview Manor was poisonous and the only place that approximated a lovely country spot was the golf course.

Kay interrupted. This was scarcely the time for cheap comedy. And besides, everyone seemed to have forgotten an important point. This was *her* wedding. *She* was the one who was getting married – not Pops or Mom. Buckley of course – but it was *her* wedding nonetheless and she didn't propose to be pushed around by *anybody*. She would marry *when* and *where* the spirit moved her. Perhaps it would be in two weeks, perhaps in six *months*.

What was more, there was no need for all this fussing. Her mother didn't need to raise a *hand* – not a finger. When she (Kay) gave the word everything would fall into place. That was the way she and Buckley were going to live. Simply and without all this *effort*. She had seen *nothing* but fuss and feathers all her life. Now she wanted no more of it. That might as well be understood.

From this point on the conversation began to resemble the Chicago wheat pit on the day of a big break. It was Buckley's first family free-for-all. Quite obviously it upset him. From where he sat, in a corner of the living room, it seemed like the breakup of basic relationships. He watched with dismay as the storm raged. Then, like a tropical hurricane, it was unexpectedly over. Instead of the tangled and broken wreckage which he had anticipated, he was astonished to learn that it had been harmoniously agreed that the wedding would take place on Friday, June 10, at four-thirty P.M. at St. George's Church.

"Are you awake?" asked Mr. Banks. "Hey, Ellie."

Mrs. Banks stirred uneasily.

"Are you awake?"

"What's the matter?" she asked, noncommitally, regarding him with one unfriendly eye.

"I've been thinking," said Mr. Banks. "I've been thinking all night. I haven't slept."

"You were snoring when I woke up," she said, without sympathy.

Mr. Banks ignored the remark. It was merely part of Mrs. Banks' morning routine.

"I've been thinking about Buckley," he said. "I'm worried. Good and worried. Do you realize, Ellie, that we know next to nothing about this boy? Just because his family has a big house and a couple of maids doesn't mean anything. What do we know about *him?*"

38

He raised himself on his elbow. "Think it over a minute. One day Kay comes home and says, 'This is Buckley. Isn't he cute? I'm going to marry him.' And we all make faces at him and dance around. But what do we *know* about him?"

Mr. Banks began to check his points on his fingers. "Has he got any money? You don't know. What's he making? Nobody knows. Can he support her? We just don't know a darn thing about the guy. He walks in the door and we hand him Kay and —"

"Darling," interrupted Mrs. Banks, "we've been through all this before. Ask Buckley. Don't ask me."

"Don't try to laugh it off." Mr. Banks was working himself into one of his pre-breakfast frenzies. "*I'm* not going to support him. Not by a damn sight. I'm —"

Mrs. Banks interrupted again. "Listen, dear. I think you're absolutely right. I've told you so every time you've brought this up. We should have found out about these things long ago. I don't know why you haven't. You've been going to have a talk with Buckley ever since Kay first told us. Sometimes I think you're a little afraid of him."

Mr. Banks snorted. "That's a fine remark, I must say. I intend to have a talk with him, all right. We might just as well have it out."

He sat on the edge of his bed radiating aggressiveness. Mrs. Banks thought he looked rather gray and tired.

By the time he reached home that evening he had decided not to make a direct approach. No use scaring the boy to death. Instead he told Kay that he wanted to have a little talk with Buckley about finances. You know – what he was earning and all that sort of thing. As a sop to liberalism he indicated that he thought Buckley was entitled to know something about *his* affairs.

Kay accepted this with irritating patience. She said O.K. if that was what he wanted. Buckley was big enough to take it. *She* knew what he was making and that should be all that was necessary, *but* if Pops wanted to go into all that old-fashioned rigamarole – O.K. She'd give Buckley the message.

Several nights later Buckley arrived for dinner carrying a bulging briefcase. Mr. Banks eyed it dubiously. What did the fellow think he was – a C.P.A.? On the other hand, if he had enough papers to fill that thing, the picture might not be as grim as he had feared. Rather decent of the boy to take it so seriously.

Mr. Banks had visualized a quiet, dignified conversation during which he would be seated in a large armchair and Buckley in a straight chair facing him. Instead he found himself sitting beside Buckley on the living-room sofa making old-fashioneds.

He finished quickly. Somehow he felt the need of fortification. After a while Ben and Tommy drifted off on their own affairs and a few minutes later Mrs. Banks and Kay disappeared in the direction of the kitchen. It was Delilah's night out. Mr. Banks was glad of this. Buckley would see that they were a quiet, simple family, well able to take care of itself, but not equipped to assume extra burdens.

They were alone. The time had come. Mixing himself another old-fashioned, he plunged.

"I guess Kay has told you," he said, "that I wanted to have a little financial chat with you." He thought this rather a footless opening in view of the briefcase resting at Buckley's feet.

"Yes, sir," said Buckley, reaching for the briefcase.

Mr. Banks raised a delaying hand. "In the old days," he continued, "fathers used to say to prospective sons-in-law, 'Are you going to be able to support my daughter in the manner to which she's accustomed?' " Unintentionally he gave a throaty laugh. Buckley did not even smile.

41

"I know what you kids are up against, though, and I've got modern ideas about these things." He stopped himself from adding, "although I may not look it."

Buckley nodded understandingly. He reminded Mr. Banks more and more of a family doctor paying a professional visit.

"What I mean is I know what you young people are up against. You all need help and I believe parents should give it as far as they are able."

"Yes, sir," agreed Buckley.

"What I was going on to say," continued Mr. Banks hurriedly, "is that parents are also up against it these days."

"They certainly are," said Buckley.

"You know what I mean — with high taxes and high prices and one thing and another."

Buckley nodded sympathetically.

"The long and the short of it is I think you're just as entitled to know where I stand as I am to know about you."

"Yes, sir," said Buckley, reaching for his briefcase.

Mr. Banks hurried on. "So here's what I propose. I'll start out and tell you a little about my own setup. You and Kay ought to know just how much you can count on us for help in the pinches — and just how much you can't.

42

Then you can go into your financial picture. How about it, eh?"

Buckley continued to regard him gravely.

"What I mean is, we ought to know about each other," added Mr. Banks.

"Yes, sir," said Buckley.

Mr. Banks took a thoughtful drink. "I've often wished my father-in-law had sat down with me before Kay's mother and I were married and told me more about himself. Young people are so apt to take things for granted and expect things that aren't possible."

"That's right," said Buckley.

Mr. Banks glanced at him quickly, but Buckley was fumbling with the catch on his briefcase.

"Well, to begin with —" said Mr. Banks nervously.

At the end of fifteen minutes Buckley knew more about Mr. Banks' affairs than Mrs. Banks had been able to dig out in a lifetime. He listened with grave attention and nodded understandingly from time to time. Mr. Banks' feeling that he was consulting his doctor became stronger as he went on. When he had finished if Buckley had pulled a stethoscope out of his briefcase and asked him to strip to the waist he would have complied without question. Instead Buckley removed a large sheaf of papers from the briefcase.

"I've brought some papers," he said, somewhat unnecessarily.

"Soup's on," cried Mrs. Banks from the living room door, in her gayest company manner. "My, you two look solemn. Come now or it will get cold."

"That's all right, my boy. We'll do your side later."

Kay jumped up from the table before they had finished dessert. "Come on, Buckley, we're late. Sorry, Mom, we promised to meet the Bakers and go to the movies. Pops kept Buckley talking too long. You don't mind if we skip the dishes do you?"

"Of course not, dear. Run along."

"Did you have a good talk with Buckley?" she asked as they cleared the dining-room table.

"Very satisfactory," said Mr. Banks moodily.

Chapter 4

THE NEWS IS BROKEN

It had been agreed that only a few intimate friends and members of the family were to be told before the engagement was formally announced in the papers. Kay said this involved a cocktail party for everyone but the relatives. She would write them when she had a chance.

The news was too big, however. It was more than she could cope with. She told everyone she met – in absolute confidence, of course – with the result that in twenty-four hours the only ones who did not know were those who would be mortally hurt if not told first.

Mr. Banks said that, under the circumstances, the cocktail party was about as necessary as a G. I.'s pajamas. Kay said that was *ridiculous*. She had only told a few people and they had *promised* to say nothing about it and *everybody* announced their engagement to their close friends at a cocktail party whether they knew about it already or *not*.

And so it was that, a few days later, Mr. Banks came out from town on the three-fifty-seven, composing an informal and, he hoped, dryly humorous little speech. It was to be about Kay as a little girl, Kay growing up and finally, in a big surprise climax, Kay announcing her engagement.

She had estimated that there would be between twenty-five and thirty people at the party. Experience had taught him that on this basis he could expect between thirty-five and fifty. In the pantry he stared with a sinking heart at the neatly arranged phalanxes of glasses that Mrs. Banks had borrowed during the day from unwilling friends. Clearly he hadn't thought this thing through. How was any one man to make drinks for a crowd like that? It would take a trained octopus.

However, this was no time for panic. Decisive action was called for. Martinis for everybody. That would be simplest. With perhaps just a few old-fashioneds ready for those allergic to gin. He pulled two large pitchers from a cupboard and went to work.

Mr. Banks was a hospitable man and in many ways a generous one. There were limits, however. He groaned with pain as he listened to one bottle after another of his best gurgle its

46

lifeblood into pitchers. But when it was all done and he stood back to inspect the result, he realized that it had been a labor of love. He cherished a special fondness for these kids who had been running through his house for twenty years and whose names he could no longer remember now that they had suddenly grown up.

The early ones were arriving. He could hear the high-pitched entrance screams of the females. He wiped his hands on a dishcloth and was about to go out and greet them when the pantry door was blocked by a rosy-cheeked young man with a disarming smile.

"How are you, sir?"

"I'm fine, how are you?" said Mr. Banks, trying to remember where he had seen him before. "Are they starting in already?"

"That's it, sir. I was wondering if I could have four old-fashioneds."

"No martinis?" suggested Mr. Banks.

"Oh, no indeed, sir. That's very kind of you. Just old-fashioneds."

Mr. Banks filled four of his emergency glasses with ice cubes and pushed them down the pantry shelf. "Thank you, sir. That's service," said the young man. His place was immediately taken by a stout youth with horn-rimmed glasses.

"Sir, four old-fashioneds and one scotch and soda."

47

"I haven't any scotch," said Mr. Banks. He hoped that his voice did not betray the fact that he had just hidden three bottles in the end cupboard behind Mrs. Banks' flower vases.

The stout young man looked nonplused. He was silent for a moment as he considered this unexpected situation from every angle.

"I don't know, sir. I guess bourbon and soda will do."

Mr. Banks, irritated by a sense of guilt, poured a highball from a bottle labeled "Whiskey – A Blend." "Wouldn't those people like martinis?" he asked.

"Oh no, sir. This is plenty."

The doorway was now filled with young men who observed him gravely. "Sir, four old-fashioneds, no garbage in two, if you know what I mean. One on the rocks and one with a dash of sugar and no bitters."

"Good God," said Mr. Banks, "do they think I'm filling out prescriptions in here?"

A tall young man with a long neck peered around the frame of the door. "Good evening, sir," he said cordially. "Looks as if it was going to be a nice party."

"I haven't seen it," said Mr. Banks testily. "What would you like? Half a dozen frozen daiquiris?"

"Oh no, sir. Just a couple of martinis."

Mr. Banks stared at him delightedly. "You mean martinis?"

"Yes, sir. Can I help you, sir? It'll speed things up a bit."

"No thank you," said Mr. Banks grimly. "I enjoy doing this. It's my hobby."

For half an hour he sloshed around frantically, trying to keep up with the demand. Then there was a sudden lull in business. "To hell with it," he muttered. Mopping his suit off as best he could, he took a martini and made for the living room, from which there now came a steady roar, like the beating of surf on rocks.

He shouldered his way into the room. Except for a few absent-minded smiles, no one paid the least attention to him. He found himself a bit of standing room in the corner by the bookcases. An intellectual type with black bangs and lovely eyes appeared before him.

"You look like a nice sort of person," she said. "Do you mind if I talk to you? I'm visiting and I don't know anyone."

"Neither do I," said Mr. Banks.

"These things can be pretty grim rat races if you don't know anybody," she said sympathetically. "I like to study types, though. Don't you?"

"It's a passion with me," said Mr. Banks.

"Have you located any?"

"Oh, sure," she said. "At a party like this it's a cinch. Now, for instance, there are just two female types here — those who are married and the still unasked. You can spot them a mile off."

"How?" asked Mr. Banks.

"Oh, it's the way they're enthusiastic about the news," she said. "You see, with the married ones it's more relief than enthusiasm. You know. Like the way you feel when somebody you're fond of, that's sort of backward, passes an exam."

"Exactly," said Mr. Banks.

"And those who are still among the unasked are full of beans in that fine old Playing-Fields-of-Eaton sort of way. You know. You're a better man than I am Gunga Din and pip pip."

"I think you've got something there," said Mr. Banks.

At this moment they were caught in an eddy that swept the black-banged girl out of sight. Mr. Banks found himself in a group which was being addressed with gestures by the stout young man with bone glasses.

"Oh, Mr. Banks. Joe's telling us a story. It's a scream. Start it again for Mr. Banks, Joe."

"Well, it's a very old story, sir. I'm sure

you've heard it. It's about a caliph's daughter."
This struck the girl beside Mr. Banks as
excruciating. She began to giggle hysterically.
"It seems that many years ago in Persia there
was a caliph who had a beautiful daughter.
Have you heard this, sir? Well, one day a
traveling salesman — "

"Stanley, where have you been? Doris and
Herbert are here." It was Mrs. Banks.

"Doris and Herbert who?" he asked.

"Well, well, well. Glad to see you, Stanley,"
boomed Mr. Dunstan. "Sorry to be late. We
got lost. Doris always insists — "

"Now go and get Doris and Herb something
to drink," said Mrs. Banks.

"Would you like a martini?" asked Mr.
Banks hopefully.

"If it's all the same to you, Stan, we'll take
old-fashioneds. Can't I help you?"

"No, no," said Mr. Banks. "It won't take a
second."

He didn't get back to the pantry a minute too
soon. A group of thirst-crazed young men were
just about to take the matter of service into
their own hands. He sent the drinks out to the
Dunstans and for the next hour he worked like
a dike mender. The only compensation was
that the guests now seemed less fussy about
what they got. The roar from the living room

51

sounded like a mob scene in a Cecil B. de Mille superspectacle.

Then the crowd began to thin. The roar subsided. He could hear the die-hards gathering in the front hall for a final stand. Mr. Banks closed down his dispensary and rejoined the remnants, outwardly a genial host, but at heart a professional bouncer.

"*You're* a help," said Mrs. Banks. "Good-by, dear. You were sweet to come."

"What do you think I've been doing? Playing pool?"

"I know. But why must you always leave the whole thing on *my* shoulders? Good-by, Helen dear. You look sweet in that hat."

He considered the first part of her remark as unjust as the last was untrue. "Where are the Dunstans?"

"They're all right. They're talking to Uncle Charlie or vice versa. Good-by, Sam. Glad you could come."

He found himself facing a blond young woman with big deer-like eyes. To his dismay she suddenly burst into tears. She was sorry, she sniffed, but this sort of thing did something to her. The thought occurred to Mr. Banks that it usually did if you took enough of it. He turned to help a highly pregnant young woman into her coat.

52

She was joined immediately by the young man with horn-rimmed glasses who appeared to be her husband. "Hi, hi," he said. "What's going on here? What's the idea? Who's leaving? Party's just warming up." He raised his glass to Mr. Banks, who noted with dismay that it was a fresh one. "Sir, the best party ever. And that reminds me, you never heard the end of that story? It was about the caliph's daughter. Remember? Well it seems a traveling salesman came to the palace. O.K., June, we'll be on our way in a minute. I just want to tell Mr. Banks something. Well, as I say, this salesman came to the palace and he fell in love with the caliph's daughter. Have you heard this one, sir?"

A carefully manicured hand plucked his sleeve. "Mr. Banks. Please. I've lost an earring and Grace can't find her gold compact and we're absolutely *sick* about it. We've looked *everywhere*. It's very peculiar."

Something in her voice gave Mr. Banks the feeling that he was under suspicion. Then he saw Mrs. Banks cornered underneath the curve of the stairs by a blond giant. She had her distress signals flying.

"Don't give it a thought," he said, patting the manicured hand. "We'll find everything later – after you've gone," he added hastily. The blond giant was explaining to Mrs. Banks how lucky any man would be to have her for a mother-in-law. Mrs. Banks was obviously lapping it up like a kitten. Yet she had called for help. Queer things, women, mused Mr. Banks, as he moved in.

Like an old cattleman cutting calves from the herd, he disentangled his guests one by one and propelled them through the front door with such light-handed skill that they were unaware of his treachery until they found themselves in the open air.

The young man with the bone glasses was still working on the story about the caliph's daughter. His audience had shrunk to his pregnant wife and Mrs. Banks, both of whom seemed to have an allergy for Oriental folklore. Placing a fatherly arm about his shoulder, Mr. Banks removed the glass from his cramped fingers.

"Good night," he purred. "Good night, my boy. You were both swell to come." As the door closed after them he instinctively placed his back against it. With a sick heart he surveyed the wreckage of what had once been his home. It occurred to him that the had forgotten to announce the engagement.

Somehow it didn't seem to matter.

Chapter 5

THE FAT IS IN THE FIRE

The only step remaining to make the whole thing irretrievable was the announcement of the engagement in the papers.

Mrs. Banks considered the wording of the notice of vital importance. Her brother, Uncle Charlie, had worked on a Chicago newspaper for several weeks when he was a boy. Since then he had been regarded as an authority on all matters concerning the press. He was now called in as a consultant.

Uncle Charlie said it didn't make a damn bit of difference how you wrote the notice. The Society Editor would hand your copy to the office boy, who would bitch the whole thing up anyhow.

Mrs. Banks pooh-poohed this. She declared that, in spite of such journalistic cynicism, this notice was going to be letter-perfect. It was written, read, re-written, reread, submitted to the Dunstan family, revised and resubmitted. There were eventually so many drafts lying around that Mrs. Banks couldn't remember which was the one that had been finally approved.

Kay was the only person who showed no interest. As long as they spelled her name with a "K" and not with a "C" she was satisfied.

Mr. Banks finally took what he hoped was the right draft down to the office to have Miss Bellamy make six copies.

Miss Bellamy was more excited about the wedding than any of the principals. She had been his secretary for fifteen years, during which she had devoted so much time to his personal as well as his business affairs that she had found no opportunity to get married herself. As a compensation she had gradually assumed remote, but nonetheless complete, control of the Banks family.

In a crisis such as this, therefore, Miss Bellamy naturally felt the weight of her responsibility. She had a real affection for Mr. Banks, but it was that of a mother for a backward son. Mrs. Banks she secretly regarded as a cultured incompetent. She had no illusions, therefore, that anything about this whole affair would be handled properly or efficiently, but she was out to do her best to pick up the pieces.

Miss Bellamy made several editorial changes in the copy without even referring the matter to Mr. Banks. Then she typed it with unerring speed. "We must read this back," she said. "There mustn't be any mistakes at this point." She read while Mr. Banks stared unseeingly at the original with fierce concentration.

"There," he said. "That's one job done as it should be." Miss Bellamy nodded understandingly. She was a great comfort to Mr. Banks. Although much too tactful to make any direct comment, she always made it quite clear to him that she knew what he was up against.

The following morning he was out of bed before the alarm went off. The morning paper lay on the door mat. He glanced up and down the shaded length of Maple Drive. Not a soul was in sight. His neighbors slumbered, unconscious of the bombshell about to explode among them.

Sitting on the bottom steps of the front stairs, he turned to the Society Section. There was Kay's face, smiling at him, and in the news column next to the picture the headline "Catherine Banks to Wed ex-Marine Officer."

He looked again. Unfortunately he had not been mistaken. It was spelled with a "C" instead of a "K." That damn fool editor. He'd go around and give him (or was it her?) a piece of his mind. In the meanwhile he had the home team to cope with.

He padded in his bare feet to the little room behind the stairs known as "The Office." Two of Miss Bellamy's copies of the release were lying on the desk. He had to force himself to look. "Mr. and Mrs. Stanley Banks of Fairview Manor announce the engagement of their daughter Catherine." How *could* Miss Bellamy! Then he remembered that he had read it back with her.

"Is it in?" Mrs. Banks was standing in the doorway.

"Yes, but they've garbled it up just as Uncle Charlie said they would. They've spelled Kay's name wrong."

"Oh, Stanley! The one thing the child —"

"I know. I know. But what can you do? That's labor for you. They don't care any more. It's the reason the country's in such a mess."

He climbed the stairs noiselessly, hoping that Kay might sleep until he was safely on the train to town.

A modern wedding is somewhat like a new theatrical production. Once the cast has been decided upon, the next thing is to determine whether it is to be Big Theater or Little Theater and then fill the house.

Kay opened the argument at dinner. "I'll tell you one thing," she said. "This is going to be a *small* wedding and a small *reception.*"

In theory this should have been music to Mr. Banks, but his trained ear sensed a discord. "I was talking to Jack Gibbons the other day," he said. "Jack's married off four daughters and he says weddings are either confined to the bosom of the family or held in Madison Square Garden."

"Well, mine is neither," said Kay. "I'm going to have my own friends and it's *not* going to be a business convention."

"I suppose I can't ask any of *my* friends," said Ben indignantly. "I suppose Tommy and I can't have —"

"Who said anything about a business convention?" interrupted Mr. Banks. "All I'm saying is you'll end up with either thirty or three hundred."

"Three *hundred!*" There was a suggestion of hysteria in Kay's voice. "Pops, if you mean that you're *crazy*. I know what you and Mom want. You want every old fogy in town so that you can hear them say. 'Yes, she really was *too* lovely. And the *most* beautiful dress, my dear.' Well I just won't *have* it. This is *my* wedding and it's going to be *my* friends."

"Listen, dear," said Mr. Banks with guarded gentleness, "this may be your wedding, but that doesn't mean it's going to be a kids' party. What do you think *we're* going to do? Leave out all our friends? Do you think we can leave out the Gibbons and the Roes and the Harts and all that crowd you've grown up with? Nonsense."

"All right, Pops. Who said you couldn't have the Roes? Molly Roe is one of my *best* friends. Of course they'd be there. But that isn't three hundred, is it?"

The argument grew more violent. Mrs. Banks was for a very small wedding to which everyone should be asked. Tommy and Ben shouted unheeded opinions. Mr. Banks pounded the table and skirted apoplexy. Kay's voice was teary. Delilah, hardened though she was to such scenes, retired to the kitchen in terror.

Mr. Banks finally had an inspiration. He fetched a yellow pad of paper from "The Office" and placed it beside his plate. On it he wrote three names.

"There," he said, "that's the smallest wedding you can have under the law — you and Buckley and the Reverend Cyrus Galsworthy. Now. Anybody else?"

Kay threw up her hands. "Really, this is so *childish,* Pops. You always get so *technical.*"

"Sometimes your father has good ideas, Kay. Go on, Stanley. Just put down the Dunstans and ourselves and Ben and Tommy."

"And Aunt Harriet, naturally, and Uncle Charlie," said Kay.

"Of course," said Mr. Banks. "But I'd go slow from there in." He wrote rapidly, keeping a tally on the side of the paper. After three quarters of an hour he ran out of sheets.

"Do you know how many people you have on the list now?"

"About fifty," said Kay sulkily.

"Two hundred and six. And that doesn't include most of our friends, and perhaps Buckley's family might have one or two people they'd like to squeeze in."

"Oh, all *right,* Pops, if you're going to be so disagreeable about it. But I tell you it's *my* wedding and it's going to be *small.* I don't *care.*"

She suddenly left the table and rushed up the stairs. Mr. Banks stared after her in amazement. "Good God, Ellie. What's the matter with Kay? We're just sitting here quietly putting down a few names and she goes all to pieces."

"She's nervous," said Tommy, through a

mouthful of cake. "All women are nervous."

Late that night, when the hush of sleep had fallen over Fairview Manor, Mr. Banks lay on his back gazing at the watery reflection of the street light on the ceiling.

Three hundred people drinking his champagne. Three hundred people eating his food. Three hundred—

He was ruined. Clearly and utterly ruined. All his life he had been a prudent and thrifty man. Now he was caught in the nutcracker of the conventions and was about to squeeze out his economic life with his own hands.

"I won't do it," he groaned, rolling onto his side. But he knew he would.

Kay was alone at the breakfast table when he came down the next morning, feeling as if he had just returned from a three-day college reunion. Looking like a May morning, she slipped a piece of bread into the toaster for him.

"Hi, Pops."

"Hi," he said gloomily. He wondered how it was that women could go through these shattering emotional scenes and bounce up a few hours later as carefree as a sea gull behind the *Queen Mary*. He watched her butter the toast and a thought began to formulate in his jaded mind.

"Listen, Kitten. I've got an idea."

"Good," she said, putting his toast on the Lazy Susan and twirling it toward him.

"I don't know whether it's good or not – and for God's sake don't tell your mother."

"Of course not. What is it, Pops?"

"I'll give you and Buckley fifteen hundred dollars to elope."

She looked at him incredulously. "Are you kidding?"

"No, honest."

"Why, Pops, you must be out of your *mind.* Elope? Not have a *wedding?* Why, I wouldn't *dream* of it! Why, you *know* Mom would *die* if I didn't have a wedding with all the trimmings. I guess I would too. Not have any *friends* to see me get married – and all the people I've grown *up* with. Why, it wouldn't be getting married, Pops. But you're just pulling my leg."

"O.K.," he said. "I just thought – O.K."

She came around the table and kissed him on the ear. "You're sweet, Pops. Only don't *stew* so much."

Chapter 6

THESE SHALL BE THE WEDDING GUESTS

"You people are looking at this whole thing upside down," said Mr. Banks. "It's not a question of how many people you *want*. You must start with the *house*. How many can stand in it at one time? The extras get jammed into the church."

After tense debate it was decided that one hundred and fifty was the absolute maximum that could be packed into 24 Maple Drive without physical injury. An additional one hundred might receive invitations to the church, but certainly not to the reception.

This did not mean, of course, that the invitations must be limited to these numbers. People living at great distances wouldn't show up if they were in their right minds, so the Bankses might as well get the credit for having asked them. Then, with any luck at all, it was safe to count on a certain number of local people being sick, or out of town, on the day of the wedding.

Mr. Banks estimated that they could rely on refusals from a third of the local invitations. On that basis, and excluding the out-of-towners, they could ask two hundred and twenty-five to both the church and the reception and one hundred and fifty additional just to the church.

To Mrs. Banks, who was used to entertaining on a retail level, this seemed like a staggering number. She proposed that each one make a separate list — just the people they *really* wanted. Then these could be combined, the duplicates eliminated — and there you were. If there were more than two hundred and twenty-five, which was unlikely, the excess could be asked to the church only.

This task occupied an harmonious evening.

Mrs. Banks jotted down the names of all living relatives (and her memory was encyclopedic), plus her special cronies in the Garden and Bridge Clubs; also all the people who had invited Mr. Banks and herself to dinner in the last few years — and whom she had neglected to ask back.

Kay put down the classmates who had written fatuous messages across her photograph in her copy of the Heathwood Hall class album, all the young men who had ever asked her to major football games, and people whom she had visited for more than two days. In a burst of gratitude she threw in the fathers and mothers of those who had put her up (or vice versa) for more than a week. To these were added her former cronies at the Fairview Manor Country Day School and sundry strays.

Mr. Banks thought in terms of old friends. As his memory limbered up, their dim forms passed before him almost faster than he could write them down. By the time he had finished with World War I his heart was overflowing with good-fellowship. Unfortunately, he couldn't remember the last names of many of them and was obliged to let them go their way. Then he could not remember where most of the balance lived (or if they did). As a result his list was a small one.

He spent the following evening combining the lists. There were alarmingly few duplications. Apparently the members of the Banks family had no friends in common. Finally he turned to his wife and daughter with a sadistic leer. "Guess how many."

Mrs. Banks squirmed uneasily. "Two hundred?" she ventured, without conviction.

"Five hundred and seventy-two," shouted

Mr. Banks triumphantly. *"Five! Seven! Two!* What did I tell you? It's either the immediate family or Madison Square Garden."

Mrs. Banks grabbed the lists. "Nonsense. Let me see. You've done something wrong. I'll bet *I* can cut this down. Now look here, we certainly don't need to have the Sparkmans. We never see them and as for that dyed-haired woman I don't care if I ever have her in my house again."

Mr. Banks wondered why it was that, every time he discovered an attractive woman, Mrs. Banks said her hair was dyed. And anyway what if it was? "Listen," he said. He was dignified now; cool, austere — and on guard. "Do you realize that Harry Sparkman is one of my most intimate friends, to say nothing of being a very good client? Why, I'd go to the ends of the earth for that fellow and he would for me."

"How ridiculous. You hardly ever see him."

"There you are," said Kay. "I *told* you these were just customers. I *knew* it."

Mr. Banks bit his lip and said nothing. He realized that he was licked for the moment. "And who in the world are the DeLancey Crawfords?" continued Mrs. Banks smoothly. "I never even heard of them."

It was Kay's inning. "Listen, Mom. How can you be so *stupid?* Don't you remember that I spent half the *summer* with them at Western Point two years ago? And Twinkey Crawford is one of my *closest, closest* friends. Why, Mother, they've been right here in this *house*. Now if we're going on like *this*, Mother —"

"Maybe they won't come," suggested Mr. Banks. "Don't they live in Pittsburgh or someplace?"   .

"We can ask those families to the church and not the reception," said Mrs. Banks, disposing of the matter.

"The *church!*" cried Mr. Banks. "you mean to say you want me to ask Harry and Jane Sparkman to the *church* and not to the *house?* Harry *Sparkman?* My intimate friend? Did *they* ask *us* just to the church when *their* daughter got married? No. And you were delighted to go to the reception. The *church!*"

The following evening Mr. Banks returned with a card file and large quantities of three-by-five cards.

"The pink are for 'Church Only,'" he explained. "The white ones are 'Church and Reception.' Now here's a rubber stamp. Whenever you're sure someone can't come because they live out of town or something, stamp that card. 'P.N.C.' That means 'Probably Not Coming.'"

68

Three nights later everyone's name had been written on a pink or a white card. The out-of-towners and the local 4Fs had been happily stamped "P.N.C." Then Mr. Banks took the second census.

Mrs. Banks watched him nervously. "Maybe they'll come out about right now," she said.

Kay looked bored. "The whole thing is just *too* sordid. I had always thought a wedding was a *joyous* occasion. The way *you're* going at it you might as well hire a couple of *bookkeepers* to put it on for you."

Mr. Banks' only reply was to count audibly to help his concentration. "Here's the box score," he announced at last. "Ten people have been asked to the church and not the reception. Five hundred and sixty-two have been asked to both. There are one hundred and fifty-two cards stamped 'P.N.C.' That leaves four hundred and ten people who might show up. Figuring that a third of them won't, you'll have two hundred and seventy-three people at the reception."

"I don't follow you very well," said Mrs. Banks in a dazed voice, "but it looks as if we'd have to cut out a few."

"All you've got to do is to throw a hundred and twenty-three people out on their necks," said Mr. Banks grimly.

Kay yawned. "I'm going to bed. *My* list is right down to the *bone*, so I can't be of much help."

Mr. Banks opened his mouth, but Mrs. Banks motioned it shut again. Kay stalked out of the room, swinging her hips with dignity.

"We can work it out," said Mrs. Banks. "Kay's upset. All we have to do is to shift these superfluous people over to the church and not invite them to the reception. Now the Harry Sparkmans —"

Mr. Banks refused the gage. The timing didn't seem right. "All right," he said. "Let's go. We'll start by putting the Garden Club in the church — and leaving 'em there."

Each white card was removed from the box, debated at length, and returned to its original place with a sigh. At the end of each round, when they came to Carlton B. Zachery, they had succeeded in eliminating or relegating to the church only a handful of names. Quite obviously they were getting nowhere. They had too many dear, close, loyal, lifelong friends, to all of whom they seemed to be indebted.

After three fruitless evenings of this sort of thing Mr. Banks had lunch with a client who was head of a large accounting firm. He had just run the gauntlet himself and, after the manner of all survivors, he liked to strut his scars. As a form of wound-licking he had reduced everything to neat figures.

Wedding guests, he explained, should be broken down into church units and reception units. That was the only way to get at the per-unit cost. At his wedding each reception unit cost $3.72, including champagne, caterers, tips, breakage, flowers, furniture-moving and extra insurance. He had not included wear and tear, feeling that, considering the occasion, it would be on the mercenary side.

Mr. Banks made some calculations on the tablecloth, and the spirit of hospitality fled from him. That evening he had a business dinner in town, but the following morning he faced the shaving mirror with the set jaw of leadership.

Someone had to take the helm. Someone had to tie up this disintegrating situation before it fell apart completely. For three seventy-two a unit he would undertake to tie up a wounded lion.

"I'll tell you one thing, Ellie," he announced as he rubbed in the shaving soap vigorously. "Only a hundred and fifty people are coming to this reception. You've got to cut down the list. I don't care who you leave out. I don't care how many just get asked to the church. Pack 'em in.

Build a grandstand in the chancel if you want. All I say is that the hundred and fifty-first person to enter this house gets thrown out on his ear even if it's your own mother."

Mrs. Banks looked at him with an astonishment that experience never seemed to dim. "Why, Stanley, that's what I said at the very beginning. And you said it was an insult to ask anybody to the church and not the reception. I'm willing enough to cut and have been right along. Now people like the Sparkmans can just as well —"

Mr. Banks winced. "It's not a question now of insulting people. It's a matter of survival. What's the world going to say when we land in the gutter just because we insisted on giving a wedding reception like a Roman emperor? No sir. It's no use arguing with me now, Ellie. I've made up my mind. One fifty is the limit."

Things looked better after he had had his breakfast, but he didn't weaken. "Now, Ellie," he said, as he left the house, "I want you to take that list today and slash it down to a realistic basis. I leave it all to you."

He felt masterful and composed that evening as he entered 24 Maple Drive. Next to achieving sudden riches, acquiring financial equilibrium is almost equally gratifying.

"Got everything fixed up, Ellie?" he called into the living room.

"Yes, only —"

"Pops." Kay came out and threw a slim arm around his neck. "Pops, you big stupid. Do you know what you did? You forgot Buckley's list. It just came today."

Mr. Banks' psyche collapsed like an abandoned bathrobe. He walked slowly to the big wing chair and sat down heavily. "How many?" he asked. His voice sounded choked.

Mrs. Banks came boiling into action beside her daughter. "He couldn't have been cuter," she declared. "He only wants a hundred and twenty-five including *everybody*. And I mean that's *everybody*. And he's marked those that he doesn't think will come — like the officers in his squadron and so on."

"Oh, they've *got* to come." Kay clasped her hands ecstatically.

Mrs. Banks hurried on. "There are about fifty 'P.N.C.s' on the list. So that really cuts it down to seventy-five. And if you figure only two thirds of those will show up —"

"O.K.," interrupted Mr. Banks firmly. "That just means cutting seventy-five more from our list. If I haven't got a friend left when this thing is over — why, I haven't got a friend left — and that's that."

All evening the list was slashed. Everyone finally got into the spirit of the thing until bosom friends were thrown out with a whoop of joy. By eleven-thirty it was reduced to two hundred and four. If a third of those didn't come there would be one hundred and fifty-three at the house. Beyond that point they could not go.

Two nights later Kay came into the living room and sat on the arm of her father's chair. She ran her fingers through his thinning hair.

"Pops darling, are you going to miss me?"

He swallowed quickly and patted her knee. "Don't let's talk about it, Kitten. If you're happy, I'm happy. That's straight."

"You're so sweet, Pops." She kissed him lightly on the forehead. "Do you know something? I hate to tell you — but I've done the stupidest thing."

"Now what have you done? Mislaid Buckley?"

"No, Pops, but for the last few days I've been thinking of people I forgot. I mean *important* people. People that I'd have simply *died* if they hadn't been at the reception."

Mr. Banks sat up suddenly, his warm mood evaporated. "How many people?"

"Oh, I *knew* you'd be cross, Pops. I know it

74

was very dumb. I'm afraid there are quite a *lot.*"

"How many is that?"

"Well, maybe forty."

From this point on morale tended to disintegrate. So did the list. Each evening, Mr. Banks thumbed through the "Church Only" cards with sad eyes.

"Bob and Liz!" he murmured. "If anybody'd told me Bob and Liz wouldn't be at my daughter's wedding reception I'd have said they were crazy. Remember the week ends we used to spend at their camp. Those were —"

"Why don't you ask them, Stan? I agree with you. It just isn't right not to have Bob and Liz. Why not make an exception?"

"Guess we should." Mr. Banks tore up the pink card venomously and carefully made out a white one. "Maybe a third of them won't come."

Or again: "Len and Louise Warner! Imagine what they're going to say. Our best friends. Three seventy-two a head. What price lifelong friends?"

"I know, dear. It's so cold and calculating when you put it that way. I should think lifelong friends were very cheap at three seventy-two a pair."

"A head," corrected Mr. Banks, transferring

the Warners to a white card.

The pink cards gradually shrank. The white ones increased daily. Mrs. Banks' apprehensive look returned.

"I just don't see what's going to happen if all these people come," she said.

"They can go out on the back lawn," said Mr. Banks.

"Suppose it rains."

"It won't," said Mr. Banks.

The day came when the list must be sent to the lady who spent her life addressing wedding invitations in a copperplate handwriting. There was a last futile attempt to get it under control.

"Who are all these clucks?" fumed Mr. Banks, pawing through the cards. "I've never heard of half of them. Here I am throwing an Irish picnic for a lot of fuddyduds I never heard of."

"Well, they certainly aren't *my* friends," wailed Kay. "You all know I wanted a small wedding with just *my* friends. Now we seem to be putting on a *convention* or something."

"I know, dear," Mrs. Banks soothed. "It's a shame we don't have a bigger house. There are a lot of people I'd like to ask, I'll admit. For instance, it seems to me we've left out all of

Mother's friends."

"Whoever these people may be," announced Mr. Banks quickly, "they are the Wedding Guests. The books are closed."

Chapter 7

YOU CAN'T WIN

It was Mr. Banks' last decisive act for many days. He and Ben and Tommy continued to live at home, outwardly just as usual, but actually more like three harmless family ghosts than active participants.

The clothes carnival was on.

Although Mrs. Banks had always contended that she never had a minute to spare from morning until night, she and Kay now rushed to town each day immediately after breakfast. Mr. Banks' socks lay undarned in the sewing bag. His buttonless shirts were stacked in neat piles in his dresser.

Each evening he and the two boys ate their dinner in glum silence while they listened to discussions of the dresses which were not there, the dresses which would have been becoming if they had been different and the dresses which would have been ravishing if Kay and her mother had been consulted about their design.

Mr. Banks gathered that the nation's dress manufacturers had suddenly gone haywire and that nothing which they had produced during the last few months would be used by a self-respecting charwoman for work clothes. He had supposed that the principal worries connected with weddings revolved around things like champagne and caterers. Now he discovered that these were small beer.

Although Kay's closet was bulging with clothes, he learned to his surprise that, for her money (or perhaps for his), it was as bare as Mother Hubbard's cupboard. Had she been Venus rising from the sea her outfitting problem could not have been more basic.

Because no one would pay any attention to him he was forced to resort to indirect methods. He would open the door of the closet and make playful remarks about the rows of dresses and shoes. He drew subtle comparisons with the children of Europe. He told anecdotes about his grandmother's frugal girlhood in a parsonage. The only recognition he received was when Kay occasionally pushed him aside with *"Please,* Pops. Can't you see you're right in the *way?* Why don't you go downstairs and *read?* You just don't *understand."*

At those moments he would be in full

agreement with his daughter for the first time in days.

Mrs. Banks' own costume seemed to be giving her a perplexing amount of trouble. She had interminable and costly telephone conversations with Mrs. Dunstan on the subject.

"What in the world has her dress got to do with yours?" asked Mr. Banks. "Are you two going as Tweedledum and Tweedledee?"

Buckley never lost confidence during these trying times. He appeared each evening like a faithful sheep dog, to spend it staring at Mr. Banks. Neither of them could think of much to say to one another so they usually listened moodily to the radio and to the undertone of women's voices from the floor above — a never-ending dialogue occasionally punctuated by screams of pleasure. At each scream Mr. Banks winced, for he knew from experience that such female ecstasy is purchased at a high price.

As time went on, however, Buckley began to show signs of alarm. He would revert occasionally to his old theme of simple weddings in little country churches. Mr. Banks said that given his choice he would pick a desert island. Once Buckley asked how much a girl — say a girl like Kay for instance — spent on clothes in the course of a year. Mr. Banks muttered something about millions. The bond of sympathy between them grew stronger daily.

Ignoring the fact that Kay and Buckley were going to live in a tiny house where Kay, at least, would spend a large part of her time with her head in the oven, she was finally outfitted for every social and sporting event that could conceivably take place between Sun Valley and Hobe Sound.

Mysterious boxes began to arrive. They appeared to be from women who did not have any last names – "Annette," "Estelle," "Helene," "Babette."

"They sound like a bunch of madams," said Mr. Banks to no one in particular.

The force of example, however, is like a mighty glacier. Mr. Banks suddenly became clothes-conscious himself. Fortunately, and unlike so many of his friends, he did not have to depend on his wedding cutaway. During those fine, flush days of the twenties he had bought a new one in order to act as best man for some backsliding old bachelor. The twenties were a long way off, however, and although Mr. Banks was proud of his figure, even he was conscious that subtle changes had taken place.

When he had last seen the suit it had been a

splendid thing — a badge of old-world aristocracy. Now it lay in an attic trunk under a hailstorm of moth balls. When Mrs. Banks finally dug it out it reminded him of something out of a sailor's slop chest.

For a long time it lay dejectedly across the chair beside Mr. Banks' bed. Each day he could think of good reasons for postponing the try-on. In the morning he was too rushed. At night he was too tired. Finally, choosing a moment when no one was around, he slipped out of his business suit and stuck a foot gingerly into a trouser leg like a bather testing the water.

Well, his legs were through at least. A bit snug, perhaps, but it might not be noticeable if he sat on the edge of things. Inhaling deeply, he sucked in his stomach as far as possible and buttoned the trousers. The effect was like squeezing the lower half of a sausage balloon.

"If any of these buttons give way they'll put somebody's eye out," he muttered, walking stiffly to the long mirror on the back of the bathroom door. Not bad for fifty, though. It was going to be a strain, of course, to keep his chest blown out like a pouter pigeon and his stomach wrapped around his back bone, but the general effect was good — like a well-preserved old oarsman.

He put on the vest carefully. The cloth

around the buttons had the strained look of a sail in a heavy blow, but if it held there was nothing to worry about.

Now for the coat. This was the crucial garment – the one which must withstand the hostile eye of the general public. Nobody looked at a man's pants. He wished the sleeves didn't fit like a freshly laundered union suit and that the back didn't make him feel as if he had been taped up by a surgeon. But these were minor inconveniences. The coat was on and holding at every seam.

Lifting his diaphragm as high as possible, he buttoned it quickly under his ribs. Mrs. Banks came in and surveyed him admiringly. "It's really wonderful, Stan. I'm proud of you."

Mr. Banks made a deprecating grimace and undid the single button of the coat. The edges parted as if they were on springs. "I think I like these coats better unbuttoned," he said thoughtfully. "You really think it fits, then?"

"Perfectly," said Mrs. Banks. "It might be a trifle snug, but that's all."

Mr. Banks continued to study himself appraisingly. "Perhaps I might manage to lose a pound or two before the wedding." He turned on her sternly. "Remember, now. From here in no more butter or potatoes or dessert."

"All right, dear. All right. But you don't need

to be so cross about it."

"Well, people insist on offering them to me," said Mr. Banks.

For some time Mr. Banks had been keeping a notebook handy for ideas about the wedding. During the day he would stop in unlikely places and jot down new items. When he went to bed he placed it on the table beside him. In the middle of the night he would suddenly switch on the light and write "confetti" or "bride's bouquet – who pays?"

The book was getting filled up now. Many of the notations were illegible. There were also numerous unexplained names and addresses which had been pressed on him by experienced friends. They were the names of people who were indispensable to weddings in one way or another, but who they were or what they were supposed to do Mr. Banks did not know.

One of the first notations in the book was the word "Champagne." It seemed a long time ago since he had written it. Life had seemed so simple and straightforward in those days. During the ensuing weeks he had received so much conflicting advice on this subject alone that he had become thoroughly confused and done nothing at all about it.

He finally stopped on his way up from the

station to discuss the matter with that *bon vivant* and connoisseur of good living, Sam Locuzos, owner of the Fairview Manor Wines and Liquor Company, whom he had been patronizing, illegally and legally, for many years.

Champagne, to Mr. Banks, was a commodity which was kept on the top shelf of the hall closet in two-bottle lots and used only on very special occasions. Sam, however, didn't have the same reverence for the stuff.

"Sure," he said. "Got plenty champagne. What kind you want? All the same. No good. Here's some. Good enough. Make it forty-five dollars a case."

Mr. Banks turned pale. "How many cases do I need?"

"How many come?"

"Oh, let's say a hundred and fifty."

"Six cases, eh?"

"Six cases! Good God, Sam, that's almost three hundred dollars."

"Sure. Got something cheaper. Forty-two dollars. No good," said Sam impassively. He was used to scenes like this. There had been other weddings in Fairview Manor.

"Tell you what," he said, and his voice was full of sympathy. "You been a good customer. I give you three bottles. Three different kinds, see. Present. You take home an' try. Then you tell me which one."

Mr. Banks watched Sam's skillful fingers as they wrapped the bottles. "There," he said. "Don't drop. An' don't forget to freeze cold. Then nobody don't taste."

"Thank you," said Mr. Banks.

On Sunday afternoon he invited two carefully selected couples to help him make the test. None of them knew anything about champagne, but Mr. Banks did not know anyone who did. He had chosen them on the theory that people who drank as enthusiastically as this group must have judgment on anything alcoholic.

They consumed the three bottles with the casual dispatch of people at a public drinking fountain. Each couple had a favorite brand of their own which they considered necessary to the success of any wedding – and it was not one of the three Mr. Locuzos had selected. They became so heated about it that everyone forgot the three empty bottles and Mr. Banks went out and made old-fashioneds. When they had gone Mr. and Mrs. Banks selected the bottle with the most impressive-looking label and let it go at that.

"Got the champagne this afternoon," remarked Mr. Banks casually to his wife that evening.

"How much did you get?"

He immediately went on the defensive. "Well, I wanted to be sure there was enough. Nothing's worse than running out the way George Evans did. Then if there's a little left over we can always —"

"But how much did you get?"

"Ten cases. But when you think —"

"Ten *cases!* How much did you have to pay?"

"Sam made me a special price. Forty-five dollars. Very reasonable."

"Forty-five dollars? For what?"

"For a case, of course. Now —"

"Stanley Banks, do you mean to tell me that you laid out four hundred and fifty dollars on champagne when you've been complaining about every cent I spent on poor little Kay for things the child absolutely *has* to have? I think it's just wicked. Don't ever speak to me again about expenses. That's all I say."

Chapter 8

BIG BUSINESS

The telephone, which had never had been an inarticulate instrument in the Banks home, now started ringing the moment the receiver was replaced in its cradle.

"Who was it, Ellie?"

"Oh, just a woman who wants to take Kay's bridal pictures."

"Some orchestra that wants to play at the reception."

"A candid camera man, dear."

"It was the little man that puts up the awning."

"Just another caterer."

"A man who wants to do the flowers."

"Only the dressmaker, darling."

What an innocent he had been! His original wedding budget had included a case or two of champagne, a couple of hundred water cress sandwiches, a wedding dress (if he was unfortunate enough to have reared a daughter who couldn't slip into her mother's), a handsome present to the bride, some miscellaneous tips and that was about all (although bad enough). The church was free. What else was there?

Now he suddenly appeared to be the sole customer of an immense and highly organized industry. He reminded himself of the Government during the war. "Keep those production lines moving for Banks. Get the finished goods to him. He's committed now. He's in this mess up to his ears. There's no drawing back. We're all behind you, Banks; behind you with caterers, photographers, policemen, dressmakers, tent pitchers — behind you with champagne and salads and clothes and candid cameras and potted palms and orchestras and everything it takes to win a wedding."

He sat in the big wing chair, shoulders slumped, staring unseeingly at the rows of books on either side of the fireplace.

"I do wish," said Mrs. Banks, "that you could arrange to meet me in town someday soon, Stanley. We've just *got* to get together with Kay and pick out the flat silver if we want to get it marked in time."

Mr. Banks regarded her with dull eyes. "The what?"

"Kay's flat silver. Her *table* silver. You know perfectly well that we give Kay her flat

89

silver and her linen."

"Her linen?" repeated Mr. Banks. His voice sounded as if he had been drugged.

"Yes, dear. Of course. Her sheets and towels and napkins and all that sort of thing."

"My God!" It wasn't an oath. It was a prayer. "Doesn't Buckley's family give anything but Buckley?"

"For an intelligent man, Stanley, you are very stupid," said Mrs. Banks.

Tommy and Ben came in. Perhaps it was just as well to let the matter drop. He looked at them closely for the first time in weeks — Ben, six feet of good looks — Tommy, a bean pole which seemed to add an inch a week. They were no longer boys but men — men ready to rear families of their own.

A warm comforting thought burst upon him and filled him with sudden peace. Soon they, also, would be getting married. Then it would be his turn to hand them over to some bride's father as *his* contribution — his sole contribution.

The only ones who seemed thoroughly immune to the situation were Kay and Buckley. As it grew more complex they grew more serene, until they seemed to Mr. Banks to be floating away like disembodied spirits, leaving the entire mess in his lap. It was a kind of spiritual sit-down strike.

"Look here," he announced sternly, "there are a lot of details we've got to talk over and I never can get you two kids together. Now I want a few minutes of your undivided attention."

But before the words were out of his mouth Kay and Buckley had drifted back into an interminable half-whispered conversation. Judging by the almost continuous giggling which rippled through it, each appeared to regard the other as a combination of Joe E. Brown and Jack Benny. Mr. Banks hated whispered conversations and detested giggling. There were moments when it seemed to him that Buckley had the most vapid expression he had ever seen on a young man's face.

"Silly ass," he muttered under his breath — and then aloud to nobody in particular, "I'm damned if I can run this circus single-handed and try to run my business too."

"*You* run it single-handed!" said Mrs. Banks indignantly. "All *you* have to do is to hand everything over to Miss Bellamy. I wish you'd stay around *here* all day. You might find out what's going on."

Basically it should have been so simple. Boy and girl meet, fall in love, marry, have babies

– who eventually grow up, meet other babies, fall in love, marry. Looked at from this angle, it was not only simple, it was positively monotonous. Why then must Kay's wedding assume the organizational complexity of a major political campaign?

Take the question of bridesmaids, for example. Kay, who had almost become a professional bridesmaid during the last five years, was now repaying her obligations with a reckless disregard for numbers.

"It's going to look more like a daisy-chain parade than a wedding," grumbled Mr. Banks as the list grew.

Fortunately, a large number were obliged to decline on the grounds of pregnancy. This reduced the length of the procession, but it did not simplify the dress problem. These must be the most beautiful bridesmaids' dresses ever worn outside of a technicolor film. They must look as if they had been snatched from Bergdorf Goodman's window, but under no circumstances must they cost a penny more than $24.50.

"They should suggest the spirit of spring," said Mrs. Banks dreamily. "Like wood nymphs in glades."

"Sort of on the idea of the White Rock girl," suggested Mr. Banks.

"*Light* green pastel with three-quarter sleeves — and a *tight* bodice and a bouffant skirt," said Kay.

"That's it," said Mrs. Banks. "And wreaths of natural flowers."

"You girls ought to work for Billy Rose," offered Mr. Banks.

Kay's face fell. "*Mom,* can you *picture* Jane Bloomer in that dress! Why, she'll look like an elephant in a *ballet* skirt. Oh, dear. This is a *mess.* Wouldn't you *know* she'd accept."

And so it went while Mr. Banks browsed absent-mindedly through the evening paper and wondered what would happen if he suddenly began to make queer noises and froth at the mouth. The incident of the champagne was still too recent, however, to make free speech advisable.

"Oh, Kay," exclaimed Mrs. Banks, "there's one thing we've forgotten. Mrs. Pulitzski. Remind me to phone her. She's simply got to be at the church to straighten you out before you go down the aisle."

Mr. Banks lowered his paper. "What's the child going to do — have the bends?"

"Oh, men never understand. Don't you see, dear, somebody's got to be there to arrange Kay's train and veil before she starts down the aisle with you?"

"I think I'll go to bed," said Mr. Banks.

It has been said that a man's home is his castle. Mr. Banks began to realize that his should have been nothing less in order to take care of the traffic that now began to flow daily through 24 Maple Drive. Joe Marvin, the architect, had certainly not designed it for a public institution.

In the pre-engagement days it had been Mr. Banks' pleasant custom to give out a cheerful "Hi" each evening as he entered his front door. And from somewhere in the house there was sure to come an answering "Hi." It was comforting and warming after an embattled day in the city.

Now, as he entered the house, he was more apt to be greeted by a din of youthful voices from the living room. There was no use calling "Hi." No one would have heard him.

It was not intentional. In fact, they were all so polite they embarrassed him. As he entered the room the young males rose in a body and mumbled something ending in "sir." Then Kay would embrace him dramatically, one foot raised slightly behind her, and say *"Pops!* We were waiting for you to make us a cocktail."

It was no time to protest. Mr. Banks would

take a hasty inventory and retire to the pantry. It seemed to him that each night another empty went into the garbage pail, where Delilah observed it glumly, brooding obviously on her rather meager salary.

Sam, of the Fairview Manor Wines and Liquor Company, became steadily more enthusiastic. "Nice wedding you have," he would remark cheerily, his deft fingers wrapping up another three bottles. "Sure I charge. Against law. You bet. Come again."

In the front hall someone was always sitting at the telephone table making a long-distance call. As far as Mr. Banks could observe none of Kay's friends had any local acquaintances. They would nod pleasantly to him as he passed.

Occasionally he would find a dime and several odd pennies beside the phone. At other times there would be a note scribbled on the memorandum pad —

Each day there were several frantic messages from Buckley's family about V.I.P.s who had been overlooked and must be invited immediately. It was Mr. Banks' job to get these belated invitations into the mailbox on the corner before going to bed. As he remembered it in after years, it seemed to him that, like a figure from a Brontë novel, he was always struggling through violent rain and sleet storms on these profitless errands.

He scuffed doggedly through unseen rain puddles. Wet branches sprang out of the darkness to slap at his eyeglasses. It would have been so easy to drop the pocketful of envelopes behind a bush and go home.

When he returned to the house he could usually hear the sound of strange bodies being disposed of for the night in various parts of the house. He used to wonder what it was about weddings that made youth so peripatetic – and where these characters would have slept on that particular night if Kay had not happened to meet Buckley.

Chapter 9

PANIC

For many years a light truck modeled along the lines of a dog-catcher's wagon and labeled "U.S. Mail," had skidded into the Banks drive each morning and delivered a stack of assorted envelopes.

During the course of breakfast Mrs. Banks had ripped hers open with an impatient forefinger, glanced at the contents and tossed them into the wastebasket. Mr. Banks, who resented anything that interfered with his morning paper, tossed most of his in without opening.

Since the invitations had gone out, however, his attitude had changed. The arrival of the morning mail was now a matter of top priority, although there didn't seem to be much family agreement on the information it contained.

"Oh, what a shame! The Lindley Davises can't come," exclaimed Mrs. Banks.

Mr. Banks' face beamed with pleasure.

"Mr. and Mrs. Throckum Nesbitt accept

with pleasure. Who in the world are Mr. and Mrs. Throckum Nesbitt? And they say if we don't mind they're bringing their daughter."

"Never heard of them. They've got the wrong wedding." Mr. Banks was fumbling with the card file. "My God, they're some people from *Pittsburgh!* We had them down as "P.N.C." Haven't they ever been asked to a wedding before? We don't even know who they are. That's some crust, I'll say. Coming all the way from *Pittsburgh!* And bringing their daughter. I'd —"

"The Cramptons are coming — oh, and the Lewises — and the Quincy Browns — and the Gaylords and — oh, how nice —"

"What's the matter? Somebody refuse?"

"No. The Whiteheads were asked to another wedding and they're giving it up because they didn't want to miss ours. How sweet of them."

Mr. Banks buried himself in the morning paper. The news from Europe was more cheering.

Each day an increasing number of people, known and unknown, accepted with pleasure. Apparently Kay had selected a day for her wedding when no one within a range of four hundred miles had anything to do. The Banks-Dunstan marriage was evidently an oasis in a desert of boredom.

Mr. Banks became increasingly impressed with the stupendousness of the spectacle which he was about to produce, and with the importance of the role which he was slated to play. It wasn't a wedding. It was a pageant. There should be an electric sign on the awning into the church:

MARRIAGE BELLS.
A SUPERCOLOSSAL SCENIC DISPLAY.
PRODUCED, DIRECTED AND ACTED
BY STANLEY BANKS.

As a form of self-torture the idea pleased him. He developed it leisurely as he composed himself to sleep that night. No one had thought of loud-speakers outside the church to take care of the overflow, or of putting the show on the air, or of billboards.

Sometime during the night he woke up filled with vague apprehension. For a few minutes he couldn't figure out what was bothering him. Then, gradually, the interior of a great cathedral took shape in his half-conscious brain. Its monolithic columns towered up and up, disappearing finally into the darkness above. The place was jammed to the doors with flashily dressed people. Somewhere an organ was thundering like a summer storm.

Suddenly the organ stopped and there was a dead silence broken only by the creaking of stiff collars and the rattle of pearls as a thousand heads turned as if on swivels to the point where he, Stanley Banks, found himself standing, quite alone, at the head of the aisle.

He tried to slip into one of the rear pews, but his feet were rooted to the floor. Then there was a series of terrific boomps from the organ and the peals of the wedding march resounded through the vaulted shadows. A shaft of white light sprang from the gloom above him and placed him in the center of a glaring pool of brilliance.

Alone, pacing slowly to the measured rhythm of the organ, he started down the aisle. It was several hundred yards long and at the end of it he could distinguish the figure of the minister which kept growing larger and larger until it towered over the whole scene and reached into the shadows — huge, sinister, forbidding, daring him to run the gauntlet.

Now he could hear titters from either side. "It's Banks. How grotesque! Why, his clothes don't fit him. Look at his figure! Why, he can't even get his coat buttoned! What a clown of a man!"

The tittering was giving way to shrieks of laughter. People were standing on the seats of the pews and pointing at him. "Look at his knees shake! He'll never make it. He'll go down in a minute. How could a man like that have such a beautiful daughter? They say she isn't his. It's a joke. He's a joke. Banks is nothing but a big fat joke – a big fat joke – a big fat joke. My God, his pants are undone!"

He was sitting up in bed. His forehead was clammy.

"Why don't you take a sleeping pill, dear?" said Mrs. Banks. "It'll quiet you down."

Of course Mr. Banks realized that this sort of nocturnal shenanigans was immature and silly. For a successful lawyer it indicated an alarming lack of self-control. However, in spite of his efforts to reason the matter through logically, he felt queasy all day. When he arrived in Fairview Manor late in the afternoon it occurred to him that it might be a good idea to go up and look at the church. Not that he wasn't thoroughly familiar with it. He merely wished to look it over in its new role as a Wedding Church.

The side door was open. The leveling rays of the late afternoon sun sifted through the stained-glass windows and filled the interior with a rich tapestry of subdued color. The place was deserted. He felt like an intruder bursting in on its introspective silence.

Standing at the head of the aisle, he studied the terrain like a hunter. Why had he thought of this intimate place as a cathedral? The pillars on either side, as he studied them critically for the first time, looked rather short and dumpy. As for the aisle, from where he stood a hop, skip and a jump would land him in the minister's arms.

"Anything I can do for you, sir?" It was Mr. Tringle, the sexton of St. George's. "Oh, it's you, Mr. Banks. I didn't recognize you. Come to look things over for the wedding? Well, don't get nervous, Mr. Banks. We'll handle everything the way you want it."

"I'm *not* nervous," said Mr. Banks irritably.

"Of course not. No sir. Some fathers get nervous, though. Good Lord, you wouldn't believe it unless you saw it with your own eyes. Fine upstanding men falling to pieces like that. Why, I've had 'em out in the vestry shakin' so's their hair was in their eyes. Shockin', some of 'em. Didn't think I'd ever get 'em down the aisle. Somethin' about the sight of a church seems to set 'em off. Seems like men's more highstrung than women that way. Everything'll be all right. Don't give it a thought, sir. Worryin' won't make it any better anyways. I can remember – Oh, have you got to go? Will

102

you go out this door please. Good night, Mr. Banks."

A short time later he found himself sitting on the living-room sofa with Kay, sipping his evening old-fashioned. Delilah was out. Mrs. Banks was in the kitchen. Kay suddenly slipped her arm through his. He patted her hand absently, his mind on Mr. Tringle.

"I know I'm a *fool*, Pops, but I want to talk to you about something. You won't think I'm *silly*, will you?"

"Of course not, Kitten. What's bothering?"

"I'm scared, Pops. Scared to *death.*"

Mr. Banks started and took a substantial swallow. "Scared? What are you scared of? Getting married isn't anything to be scared of. Marriage is the most normal —"

"Oh, Pops, I'm not scared of *marriage*. It's much sillier than *that*. You see —" He always had a particular yen for Kay when she said "You see" and snuggled.

"It's this way, Pops. You know how I wanted a *simple* wedding — out in the country some-where. Well, that's *out*. We don't *live* in the country. Period. But this thing is getting bigger an' bigger an' *bigger*. Oh, I know it's un-grateful, Pops. You're wonderful. But some-times it scares the living daylights out of me."

Mr. Banks glanced toward the kitchen and dropped his voice. "You mean like going down the aisle?"

"Every time I *think* of it, Pops, I turn into a cold sweat. Suppose my *knees* got shaking just as I started. And suppose they shook so finally that they let me down *entirely* and you had to *drag* me to the altar like a sack of *meal.*"

Mr. Banks regarded her for some moments with despair in his eyes. "We might both have a short snort just before the show starts," he suggested finally, but without conviction.

"*No* sir. That won't do, Pops. I'm not going to blow gin in the minister's face at my own wedding."

"I was thinking of a whiskey and soda," said Mr. Banks. Then he pulled himself together with an almost visible effort. "Listen, Kitten. Get this into your head. There's nothing to worry about. See? *Nothing* to worry about. All your life when you've been bothered *I've* been there, haven't I? Well, I'll be there when that wedding march starts. All you've got to do is to take my arm, lean on me and think about how you're the most beautiful bride in the world and how proud I am of you. That's all. Just relax. I'll do the rest."

"Oh, Pops!" Kay was looking at him with

loving reverence. "You *are* wonderful. *Nobody* could be scared with you. Nothing *ever* fazes you, *does* it, Pops?"

Chapter 10

IT IS EASIER TO GIVE THAN TO RECEIVE

Anyone faced with the necessity of giving a wedding present should remember that only the first few to arrive will receive the admiration they deserve. Shop early and avoid oblivion.

The first present came two days after the engagement had been announced in the papers. It was a hand-painted tray. Mrs. Banks had cleared out the spare room and set up, against the wall, a card table covered with her best tablecloth. Kay placed the tray on it like an acolyte arranging an altarpiece, while the family gathered reverently around. The boys became a bit shy and treated Kay with a new respect.

For a few days it looked as if the first present might achieve the double honor of being the last as well. Then they began to move in; a thin trickle at first, growing steadily to a mighty stream. Mrs. Banks borrowed more card tables. Kay fluttered over them like a maternal barn swallow.

The Banks family had not yet become accustomed to endless bounty. That someone should take the trouble to go out and purchase with hard money a gift of any sort, still filled them with tender gratitude. Regardless of merit, utility or beauty, these first presents were snatched from their wrappings with cries of wonder and delight.

What puzzled Mr. Banks was that neither Mrs. Banks nor Kay ever forgot a detail in connection with any gift. For twenty-three years he had been impressed by the fact that neither of them seemed capable of grasping or retaining the most elementary details. Mrs. Banks could never remember, for example, whether the mortgage company owed Mr. Banks money or vice versa, and Kay still thought that the Rubaiyat was a toothpaste, but when it came to the matter of wedding presents, their donors and their sources, they both had memories like rogue elephants.

In an attempt to show paternal interest Mr. Banks tried to compete during the early days. By occasionally visiting the spare room for a private refresher course he was in control of the situation up to the thirty-sixth present. Then, while he was at the office one day, Mrs. Banks borrowed three more card tables and shifted everything around.

After that he struggled for a short while, then gave up. He never forgot the first thirty-five presents, however. Occasionally he tried to establish himself by picking up some object from this restricted group and remarking, "This bowl from the Appleblossoms is a nice thing." No one paid any attention to him, but it made him feel that he still had a stake in the situation.

At first he had taken special pleasure in the drinking merchandise. This department led off with a dozen old-fashioned glasses. Then came ditto highball glasses. A cocktail shaker from Steuben, he was chagrined to note, was better than anything of the sort he had ever owned or probably ever would. A gleaming copper bar-table with red leather side rails filled him with envy.

Time passed and in its course Kay accumulated three dozen old-fashioned glasses, two dozen glass muddlers, four dozen highball glasses, three large cocktail shakers, two martini stirrers, two bride and groom midget cocktail sets, two whiskey decanters, five silver bottle openers, a half acre of wineglasses, a portable bar and sundry jiggers and cork-screws. The place began to look like a setup for *The Lost Weekend*. Mr. Banks' connoisseur's enthusiasm was displaced by misgivings.

He was no teetotaler. On the other hand he now began to wonder whether he possibly had not overdone things a bit and conveyed to the world the impression that he was rearing a brood of alcoholics.

Given enough ointment there is always a fly. Given enough presents there is always One-of-Them. They are as inevitable as death. The only thing that is unpredictable is the direction from which they come. Kay's arrived one Saturday in a large wooden box, buried deep in Its nest of excelsior as if trying to hide Its shame.

It was a china lad in a china pink coat and a china maid in a Harlem pink skirt, crossing a china bridge which did not bridge anything, on Harlem blue china feet. As It rose from Its hiding place the family looked at It in stunned silence as the crew of a South Seas whaler might have watched a sea serpent emerge from the waters beside the ship. They knew, without the necessity of words, that this was IT.

Mr. Banks was the first to recover himself. "Who?" he demanded through clenched teeth.

They pawed through the excelsior and fished out a card. "With love and affection from Aunt Marne."

A composite sound came from the Banks family. It was the cumulative cry of man's frustration through the ages. It might have been made by a Neanderthal father who, returning to his cave, finds a saber-toothed tiger licking his whiskers at the entrance.

Aunt Marne, of all people! The one member of the family who had been counted on to come across handsomely — preferably with a substantial check! She was rich, she was unmarried and she spent a week with the Bankses each fall. When Mr. Banks thought of all the evenings he had spent listening to Aunt Marne's non-stop chatter he was sorry he had not given way to his instincts while the opportunity was at hand and regardless of the consequences.

This was the Great Betrayal. From now on the name of Aunt Marne would be coupled with those of Judas Iscariot, Brutus, Benedict Arnold and Tojo.

"What are we going to *do* with it?" wailed Kay.

"Do you want me to tell you?" asked Mr. Banks.

Mrs. Banks examined it at arm's length. "I

suppose we'll have to put it with the other presents. She's apt to come popping in any time."

"Perhaps we could change it" – hopefully.

"I've been looking. It doesn't say where it came from."

"It would be a pity to drop it," said Mr. Banks.

They put It on a card table in a far corner. They tried It on top of a chest of drawers. They hid It on a window sill behind an electric clock. No matter where they placed It, It was the first object which struck the eye when one entered the room.

The visitors' opening gambit was unvaried. "My *dear*, I never saw so many lovely presents." Then they would walk straight to the Thing and stand before It, picking up little objects in the neighborhood and laying them down. It was only a matter of minutes before they would have their hands on It. Operating on the theory that offense is the best defense, Mrs. Banks stepped in at this moment and explained that it was all a huge practical joke. Once they knew how excruciating it was everyone laughed heartily, but there was a malicious note in their mirth that Mr. Banks did not like.

Life was never quite the same after the

arrival of Aunt Marne's present. Gone now the simple note. Gone the spirit of guileless appreciation for a gift as such. Gone the impartial screams of pleasure as the wrappings fell away. He who deceives a trusting dog does harm. From this point on the contents of each incoming package were appraised with the cold commercialism of an Oriental bazaar.

"What is it?"

"Another tray."

Deep groan from Kay. "It's a stinker, too."

"We can take it back. Where's it from?"

"The Tucker Gift Shop."

"We have almost enough junk from there, darling, to get something you really want."

"The trouble is there's nothing in the Tucker Gift Shop that *anybody* wants."

Mr. Banks, the erstwhile cynic of the family, found himself cringing in the face of this cold brutality. His heart went out in sympathy to the army of breadwinners who would soon be tearing out what little hair was left over the bills from the Tucker Gift Shop.

"That's a *nice* tray," he would remark fatuously. "What's the matter with it? There are lots of girls would give their eyeteeth —"

"Oh, Pops, you don't know anything *about* it. Let them *keep* their teeth. They can have it for nothing."

Mr. Banks hated to see Kay get hard.

Someone had given Kay a Bride's Book for an engagement present.

A Bride's Book is, to a prospective bride, what a score card is to a baseball fan. The statistics are as important as the game itself. Kay's book was bound with white satin, already autographed with her thumb prints. It contained a quotation from Longfellow on the title page.

O fortunate, O happy day
When a new household finds its place
Among the myriad homes of earth.

Mr. Banks read this several times with interest. To him it put Longfellow in the running with the prophet Isaiah. Anybody who found a place for a new household in this cockeyed world would not only be fortunate and happy, but also shot in the pants with luck. Nevertheless, he thought it struck rather a gloomy note for a book of this kind.

But Kay wasn't interested in housing. Her competitive sense was aroused by the blank pages for listing each present and the name of the donor. A number was printed before each entry space, and in the back of the book were perforated sheets of corresponding gummed numbers to be pasted on the presents.

Kay had examined these sheets immediately to be sure there were enough numbers to meet her estimates. Although her memory for figures was notoriously bad, she knew exactly how many presents each of her friends had received since Sally Gross had led off the bridal procession five years ago.

Booboo Batchelder had held the record for the last two years at 234. Her friends had always regarded it as unfair competition inasmuch as Booboo's father had once been a Senator. But statistics were statistics nevertheless.

Kay made no predictions. She was an ambitious young woman, however, accustomed to setting her sights high. Her motto was "235 or bust." She had no Senator father to fall back on, but she had built up a clientele of her own over the years. From her point of view at the moment quality or desirability did not matter. It was quantity that counted.

True to the American tradition, the receiving of gifts, which had been started so simply and spontaneously, soon developed into an organized industry in which each person became a specialist.

Mr. Banks' field was the disposal of empty

cartons, wrapping paper and excelsior. No one appointed him to this important work. It merely seemed to fall to his lot by a process of natural selection.

Being a thrifty man, when left to his own devices, he foresaw a vague future use for all this material. He cleaned out a corner of the cellar by consolidating other objects for which he also had a vague future use.

Each day the debris was piled waist-high in the back hall. One by one he bumped the cartons down the cellar stairs, sorted out the wrapping paper, jammed the excelsior into a special box and nested the empties neatly.

The corner filled rapidly and, as the boxes began to cover the entire cellar floor, his system broke down. Now he merely stuffed the loose debris into the cartons, carried them to the foot of the stairs and kicked them toward the nearest available space. The restoration of order was clearly something to be deferred for a rainy Saturday afternoon. Ultimately his chief problem was to keep a passageway open to the oil burner.

His task would have been dull, but relatively simple, had it not been for gross inefficiency in the higher echelons.

"Mother, what in the *world* did you do with that box from Rose Wood?"

"You mean the one with the tumblers?"

"Yes."

"Why, I don't know, dear. I suppose I put it in the back hall."

"But, *Mother*, I hadn't finished *unpacking* it. I was called away. I *do* wish, Mother —"

"Your father will know, dear," said Mrs. Banks soothingly, going to the head of the stairs.

"Stanley."

"Yes?"

"Did you notice that one of those boxes you took down to the cellar wasn't quite unpacked?"

Mr. Banks put down his newspaper. "Now listen, Ellie —"

"Well, won't you just run down in the cellar and have a look, dear. It's a box from Scranton. Just bring it up and we'll go through it up here."

Or again: "Darling, I'm afraid we've left a card somewhere in one of the boxes. A set of beautiful salad plates came and we don't know who sent them. Are you sure there wasn't a card in one of those cartons you brought down?"

Mr. Banks admitted that it was barely possible that he had carried a card down to the cellar without noticing it.

116

"Well, won't you try and find that box, dear, and just run through it. It was from the Tucker Gift Shop, so it ought to be easy."

Mr. Banks returned to the cellar. The place began to remind him of the hold of a badly packed cargo ship. Which boxes had come today, which yesterday or which a week ago was any man's guess. And half of them were from the Tucker Gift Shop.

He plunged his hands into the nearest carton, came up with an armful of paper shavings and tossed them moodily onto the concrete floor. Half an hour later he reappeared dragging streamers of packing from either ankle.

Mrs. Banks called to him from the living room. "Oh, Stanley. Thanks, dear. Kay found the card. It was stuck between two plates. Mrs. Morley sent them. Wasn't that sweet of her?"

"I'm going to take a bath," said Mr. Banks.

The present-gazers began to arrive now in substantial numbers. Although their words were floated on milk and honey, they were obviously there for one or all, of four purposes:

1. to see how their present stacked up with those of their competitors;
2. to find out if it was being given a

favorable display position;

3. to judge if Kay was faring better in either quality or quantity than their recently married daughter;

4. to pick up ideas for cheap presents that look expensive.

Mrs. Banks, having been a present-gazer for years, knew only too well the importance of position. She became an expert at juggling the arrangement of the objects on the card tables. While she engaged her guests in animated chatter her eyes were on the door and her fingers were moving ceaselessly about the tables. As a result, by the time a donor moved across the room he would find his gift enshrined between Kay's flat silver and the super-de-luxe china from Aunt Emily.

It was a woman's world. Accompanying male present-gazers appeared only between five-thirty and seven. They would totter around the room behind their female convoys, staring over their shoulders with codlike eyes, until Mr. Banks took pity on them and put drinks into their hands. As their vicelike fingers closed over the cool, moist surface of the glass they would look at him gratefully murmuring, "Oh, I really don't want this. Thanks."

At this point male gazers abandoned all

further attempts to examine presents. Mr. Banks talked to them at the other end of the room until their knees began to sag. Then he converted the living room into a kind of crèche and spread them around in vacant chairs until they were called for.

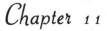

GENTLEMEN'S CATERERS ALL ARE WE

"We must do something about the caterer," said Mrs. Banks.

"The what?" Mr. Banks understood perfectly.

"Darling, did you think Delilah was going to handle the wedding reception all by herself?"

Mr. Banks couldn't truthfully say that he had thought about the matter at all — or that he wanted to think about it now.

"I've been finding out about caterers," continued Mrs. Banks in the bland tone of one conscious of having done her work while others fiddled. "The only thing to do is to have one come out from town. Sally Harrison had one for little Sally's wedding. She was crazy about him. His men were efficient and courteous and he's done a lot of weddings for

120

people we know so he understands the sort of thing we want and she said he was very reasonable. Let's see. She gave me a card. I put it somewhere. Now let me think—"

Mr. Banks picked up his book, knowing that he wouldn't be troubled by the subject again for at least half an hour.

On the following Saturday morning Mr. and Mrs. Banks drove to town and visited the offices of Buckingham Caterers, specialists in luncheons, dinners, buffet suppers, cocktail parties, wedding receptions, christenings, lodge meetings and general social functions.

Mr. Massoula, who appeared to be in charge, was obviously a young man who knew his way about. He had a long upper lip decorated on its lower edge with a tiny mustache, reminiscent of a fringe on a lamp shade. His double-breasted, blue suit was sharply creased and his thin, black hair was plastered down so tightly that it might have been painted on his skull.

Wedding reception? Yes indeed. Buckingham Caterers were fully equipped to take the whole affair over. Mr. and Mrs. Banks didn't need to give the matter another thought. Just specify the date and they could romp off to the Arizona Biltmore or Palm Beach or Palm Springs or wherever it was that people like Mr. and Mrs. Banks spent their time. The point was they *did not need to worry.*

Buckingham Caterers had handled some of the biggest and most expensive weddings in the country. Mr. Massoula let it be understood clearly that they were not in the habit of putting their shoulder to weddings which were not in the upper brackets of the social scale.

"But first," said Mr. Massoula, reaching under the table and producing several large photograph albums, "I'd like to get your ideas about a wedding cake. Once the wedding cake has been established Buckingham Caterers take over. Now here is a very popular cake. That's Brenda Santanya. You know. Daughter of Princess Fraschisi by her second husband."

Mr. Banks looked at his wife. They hadn't even thought about a wedding cake. To Buckingham Caterers it was obviously not a matter for discussion. Mr. Massoula turned over dozens of photographs showing brides and grooms about to destroy hideous cakes of every size and shape. One could see that the cakes were different, but the brides and grooms all looked alike.

Mr. Massoula had an encyclopedic memory for names and social connections. The First Families of the nation passed in review before Mr. and Mrs. Banks. They had never heard of most of them, but they were pleased by the way that Mr. Massoula assumed that all these people were their buddies.

"That's one of Tommy Manville's weddings," he said. "We've done almost all of them. Good old Tommy. Delightful person, isn't he?"

Mr. Banks was about to say "Yes" but checked himself. He began to wish he had chosen a less socially prominent caterer.

"Ours isn't going to be a big reception," he ventured.

"Small and select. I understand perfectly. Buckingham Caterers can handle them any size."

Mr. Banks' fingers tightened on the edge of the table. "We don't want a cake," he said with dignity. Mrs. Banks' admiring glance fortified his courage.

"What! You don't want a cake! Why —"

Mr. Banks shot the works. "I think cakes are cheap," he said. "Every Tom, Dick and Harry has cakes. We don't want one."

Mr. Massoula looked at him with new respect. "I understand," he murmured. "It is true that the *very* select weddings no longer have them. We must show them, though. Most people wouldn't understand if we didn't."

"Of course not," said Mr. Banks. He dreaded the moment when he had to tell Mr. Massoula that this particular reception was to be held in a place called Fairview Manor.

Mr. Massoula brought up another large album from under the table. "While you're here I'd like to have you look at a few shots of some of our receptions."

As he looked Mr. Banks' dismay turned to panic. Buckingham Caterers not only dealt exclusively with the uncrowned heads of American Industrial Aristocracy, but apparently they catered only on huge estates and in palaces. He wondered how he could get out of the whole thing gracefully. Maple Drive had suddenly become a kind of suburban back alley. Quite obviously his home would look like somebody's gatehouse to Mr. Massoula.

But it was too late. Mr. Massoula had pulled out a pad of forms. "Now we should get some idea of what you would like to serve. We will supply the champagne of course."

Much to his chagrin Mr. Banks turned slightly red. "I'm sorry. What I mean is I didn't know. That is to say I've bought the champagne already."

Mr. Massoula's face clouded with politely restrained annoyance. "Then we will have to charge corkage, of course."

"Corkage?"

"A dollar a bottle for drawing and poring."

"Oh, Delilah can take care of all that."

"If you are referring to one of your house staff," said Mr. Massoula firmly, "you must understand that in an affair of this kind the caterer takes over completely. Any other arrangement would cause friction in the servants' quarters. I am sure *you* understand, madam." He smiled at Mrs. Banks as mothers smile at one another over the heads of their wayward young.

Mrs. Banks returned the smile. "Indeed I do."

"By the way," said Mr. Massoula, "are you serving French champagne?" Had he said, "You are serving French champagne, of course?" the meaning would have been the same.

"As a matter of fact I'm not," said Mr. Banks in a tone that acknowledged the eccentricity of his decision. "I just think it's a shame to waste good vintage champagne on these kids. So I'm giving them American," he finished lamely.

Mr. Massoula nodded understandingly. "That will be all right with us," he said graciously. "Now, about the food. Let's see. The wedding is in early June. How about a large cold salmon at either end of the table with the various salads in great bowls at the center? Another dramatic arrangement is cold

125

sturgeon in the middle of the table. Now for the ices, we pride ourselves on a very special effect with colored electric lights embedded in a huge cake of ice, capped —"

"But," interrupted Mrs. Banks timidly, "we hadn't intended to have that kind of a reception."

Mr. Massoula gave her a puzzled look and laid down his pencil. "What did you have in mind, madam?"

Mrs. Banks fingered her handbag nervously. "Well, we thought that maybe some small assorted sandwiches — different kinds, you know — and ice cream and little cakes —"

"Of course you can have what you wish, madam, but that is usually what we serve at children's parties."

"Well, it's what we *want*," said Mrs. Banks with a sudden harshness that in turn surprised her husband.

"Of course. Of course," said Mr. Massoula, making notes. "And I can assure you that you will be pleased when you see the results. Now where will the reception take place?"

"Twenty-four Maple Drive, Fairview Manor," said Mr. Banks belligerently.

"Is that a club or a country estate?" asked Mr. Massoula.

"It's my *home*," replied Mr. Banks with dignity.

126

Mr. Massoula bowed slightly in deference to the generic sacredness of all homes. "What attendance do you anticipate?"

"About a hundred and fifty."

"Is it a large house?"

"No," said Mr. Banks defiantly. "It's a small house."

"Then of course you are planning for a marquee on the terrace."

"I have no terrace. If they overflow the house they can tramp around in the yard."

"And what if it rains?" asked Mr. Massoula with a rising inflection, glancing at Mrs. Banks. "What if it pours that day?"

"That's just what *I* said," put in Mrs. Banks. "Stanley, what *would* we do if it poured?"

"A marquee is very inexpensive," reassured Mr. Massoula soothingly, "and even if it doesn't rain you really *should* have it. I'll tell you what we'll do. I'll have one of our field engineers go over the property. We always have to do that anyway to study circulation problems and that sort of thing."

"Listen," said Mr. Banks desperately. "We've talked about everything but how much this is going to cost."

"The cost," said Mr. Massoula, "will be relatively small for a party such as you describe." IIis tone indicated that the kind of

127

party which Mr. Banks had described wasn't much of a party. "For the *minimum* refreshments which you have specified the cost will be a dollar and a half a head, plus corkage, plus the cost of the marquee and sundry small expenses. For that Buckingham Caterers take *complete* charge, including experienced and courteous men who have been with us for years. Don't consider the cost, Mr. Banks. It will be trifling compared to the service which you will receive."

Apparently the social season was dragging a bit, for a few days later Mr. Massoula arrived in person at 24 Maple Drive. He was accompanied by a sheepish-looking character with handlebar mustaches, whom he referred to as Joe. Mrs. Banks assumed that he was one of the field engineers whom Mr. Massoula had spoken about, although he looked more like a horsecar conductor.

Mrs. Banks was a meticulous housekeeper and she had always been proud of her home. Now, as Mr. Massoula and Joe wandered from room to room with cold appraising eyes and occasional mumbled comments, she realized that neither of them had ever before catered in such a hovel.

"Small," said Mr. Massoula.

"I'll say," agreed Joe. "How many head did you say?"

"Hundred fifty."

"Jesus," said Joe. Mrs. Banks was afraid he was going to expectorate, but he refrained with an obvious effort.

"Circulation's bad," said Mr. Massoula.

"I'll say," agreed Joe.

"We'll have all the windows open on that day," assured Mrs. Banks.

"What *we* mean by circulation," said Mr. Massoula kindly, "is the *guest* flow from room to room. A room with two interior doors has minimum circulation. A room like this with only one is – is – well, it's a death trap. Where does this go?"

Mr. Massoula pulled the knob of a door. It came off in his hands.

"I'm so sorry," said Mrs. Banks miserably. "It does that unless you push it in first. That just goes into a closet anyway."

Mr. Massoula placed the knob on the dining-room table. "Is this the pantry?" The two men seemed to fill the little room.

"Small," said Mr. Massoula.

"Dark," said Joe.

Mrs. Banks snapped the electric switch. Nothing happened.

"Bulb's busted," said Joe. "I seen enough."

Mrs. Banks followed them gloomily back to the living room.

"Circulation in this room's O.K.," said Mr. Massoula.

"Only one that is," said Joe.

"But you couldn't get more than a hundred and twenty-five in the house."

"Squash 'em like bugs if you did," said Joe.

"I'm planning to take a lot of these things up to the attic, you know," explained Mrs. Banks. "All those straight chairs go up, and the small tables and standing lamps, and we're thinking of taking up the rug."

"Takin' th' rug up ain't goin' to give any more room," said Joe. Mr. Massoula maintained a displeased silence.

"Have you any suggestions?" asked Mrs. Banks nervously.

"Yes, madam, I have," said Mr. Massoula. "Even with a marquee you're going to be cramped. By the way, Joe, go out in the back and measure for the marquee. Now you see, madam, circulation's your big problem. The first thing you've got to do is clear this room of *all* furniture."

There was a suggestion of tears in Mrs. Banks' voice. "You don't mean the big davenport and the armchairs and —"

"Of course. *And* the piano. *Everything* must

come out of this room. Now in the dining room —"

"Does the dining-room table have to go too?" she wailed, but Mr. Massoula was not listening.

"That chandelier over the dining-room table — could that be looped up or something?"

In view of the fact that the chandelier was not made of rubber tubing Mrs. Banks did not see how it could.

"Then you better have the electrician take it out an' cap it temporarily," said Mr. Massoula. "It's in the way. Now about these doors between the rooms. They've got to be taken off. You'd be surprised to see how much circulation you lose on account of doors. Especially doors like these."

Mrs. Banks might have forgiven him if he had not added that last sentence. As it was she lost her temper as an alternative to tears. "What in the world do you think I've got upstairs — a cold-storage warehouse? And who do you think is going to lug all this stuff up there — if there was a room? And who do you think is going to get it down again?"

But Mr. Massoula was a creative artist. Details were not in his line. "We'll connect the marquee to this French door from the living room," he said. He tried to open the door but it merely slammed violently back and forth at the top. The bottom was apparently glued to the sill.

"It's stuck," explained Mrs. Banks. "I've been meaning to have that door fixed."

Mr. Massoula opened a window and leaned out. "Hi, Joe," he bawled. "Figure on a connecting angle through the French door here. Measure from the outside. The thing's stuck."

"I'll say," came an angry voice from the lilacs. "Too many God-damn bushes out here. Ought to get rid of 'em."

Chapter 12

TOMORROW'S MY DAUGHTER'S WEDDING DAY

The day before the wedding came at last.

When one concentrates fiercely and at length on an event in the distant future it eventually becomes fixed in the mind as something forever remote. As a result it is a shock to awake some morning and find that the distant future has suddenly become the immediate present. It is like a foolish rumor about a lion in the district, which no one takes seriously until the beast springs at you from behind a lilac bush.

The wedding rehearsal was scheduled for five-thirty. Mr. Banks set out for the office exhibiting a nonchalance that he did not feel. Yes, of course, he would take the three-ten from town. There was nothing to get so excited about. Beneath the surface, however, he was distinctly nervous. He felt like a man moving beneath powerful floodlights.

The floodlight operator must have been off duty during his trip to town, however. The same apathetic faces greeted him at the station with the same apathetic comments about the weather, their health, or their lack of it. As the train pulled out of Fairview Manor, Reggie Fry lurched into the seat beside him and spent three stations describing an intricate real-estate deal in the course of which he had outwitted and discomfited the best brains in the business. Mr. Banks could stand it no longer.

"My daughter's getting married tomorrow," he said simply.

"Really?" said Mr. Fry. "Didn't know you had a daughter. Time flies, eh? I hope she's got a place to live after she's married. It's a bad situation. Getting worse. The Real-Estate Board put out some interesting figures about it in their last bulletin. I've got it here somewhere. Here it is. Now just let me read you these few paragraphs. This is on the volume of building of one-family homes in the mid-continent states during the first quarter."

Mr. Banks shuddered and gave himself up to his thoughts.

He would have found it hard to describe just what he expected when he arrived at the office.

Obviously he had not anticipated organized cheering as he came in the door, yet it depressed him to have Miss Rooney nod to him from the switchboard and say, "Morning-MrBanksnicemorning," just as she did on the other three hundred working days of the year.

Even his partners failed to grasp the significance of current events. As each one drifted into Mr. Banks' office during the morning he offered some fatuous remark about not falling down in the aisle or trying to bend over in his cutaway. Then, having made their concessions to the trivia of life, they concentrated on the task of dumping on his desk every unanswerable and boring problem they could dig out of their pending files. They reminded Mr. Banks of executives cleaning out their desks before leaving for their summer vacations.

During the moments when his partners were not bedeviling him the outside world took up the torch. The cream of the dullest and most long-winded of Mr. Banks' clients flocked into his office for no other apparent reason than to make sheep eyes at him and fill up an idle hour with the sound of their own voices.

The only positive note was the telephone. Whenever Mr. Banks thought about that morning during later years it was his telephone buzzer which sounded the motif of the nightmare cacophony.

"Darling, the worst thing. Old Mr. McQuade is down at the station. – McQuade, dear. *I* don't know. He's some relative of *yours.* – Well, it's no use arguing about that *now.* He's down at the station and he wants to know where he's supposed to *go.* Where in the world am I going to put him?"

Only the presence of a customer mooning beside his desk restrained Mr. Banks from detailed instructions.

"Hello. Is this you, Stanley? – This is Ella. *Ella.* – Is this Stanley Banks? – This is *Ella.* Yes. How *are* you? We came down the last minute as a surprise. Now we don't want you to bother your *head* about us. Just tell us how the trains run to Fairview Manor and how to get from the station to your house. If you haven't room to put us up we can go *anywhere* at all. The last thing we want to do is put you to any trouble. I guess you've got troubles enough just now." (Hysterical laughter.)

The sheep-eyed gentleman beside Mr. Banks' desk looked at him anxiously. "I hope that wasn't bad news," he said.

"No, no," said Mr. Banks. "I've got a daughter getting married tomorrow."

"Oh, of course. Quite," said the sheep-eyed gentleman and resumed his narrative.

"Darling, I'm so sorry to bother you again but I'm almost crazy. You can't imagine what's happened. The Bennett boy has come down with measles and they can't take in Cousin Laura and Bob. What in the *world* are we — I know, dear, but I thought you might have some *ideas.*"

By twelve-thirty he could stand it no longer. Shoving a pile of papers into a desk drawer, he rang for Miss Bellamy. "I'm getting the hell out of here," he said defiantly. The phone rang. "I'm gone."

"So sorry," murmured Miss Bellamy into the mouthpiece. "He was called away very hurriedly. He just this moment left the office. No, I don't think I could catch him. I know how sorry he'll be. He wanted to talk to you. Yes, I'll certainly tell him." She hung up the receiver. "It's that Mr. Wadley you've been trying to get for three days."

"That fellow has no judgment," said Mr. Banks.

"Yes indeed," said Miss Bellamy soothingly. "Now I have everything ready in this envelope. Here's a list of all the ushers and bridesmaids and where they're staying and their telephone numbers. And then here's a full set of church seating lists. There's one for each usher with his name typed on it and special instructions

137

for those who have special jobs. I've put in some extra copies just in case. Oh, yes, and I've phoned all the papers just to make sure they remember and — well — I guess that's all till I see you in church."

Miss Bellamy looked suddenly deflated and wistful. Mr. Banks had never seen her like that before. For one terrible moment he thought she was going to cry.

"You've been wonderful," he said awkwardly. "Wonderful. I'll never forget it." He left quickly as the phone started to ring.

Several days earlier Miss Bellamy had sent crisp little notes to all the ushers and bridesmaids, attempting to impress upon their scattered minds that the rehearsal would be at five-thirty at St. George's Church and the importance of being prompt.

Mr. Banks had insisted on being there fifteen minutes ahead of time. He wanted this wedding well rehearsed — no sloppy business — and he felt somehow that if he and Mrs. Banks were early it would expedite things. To his dismay he found the church in complete darkness. The Reverend Mr. Galsworthy and the organist were nowhere about. The smoothly functioning machinery of St. George's was at dead center and the self-starter was missing.

Mr. Banks had pictured the organist busily warming up his instrument with a burst of arpeggios and Mr. Galsworthy nervously pacing the aisle, measuring distances, putting markers in his book and making a few final notes. Not even Mr. Tringie, the sexton, was puttering around.

He finally located Mr. Tringle in the cellar of the rectory gluing the back of a broken chair. "Good gracious," he exclaimed. "That late a'ready? Maybe we best go up an' put on the lights."

The first bridesmaid turned up at a quarter to six. She was a wispy little number who seemed to have been left out of everything to date and was obviously terrified at the thought of what lay ahead. The organist strolled in several minutes later.

"Are you sure," asked Mrs. Banks anxiously, "that you know what you are going to play at the wedding?"

"Oh, yes," said the organist. He was an earnest-looking young man with heavy horn spectacles. "Oh, quite. This is the Broadhurst wedding, isn't it?"

The knuckles of Mr. Banks' hand grew white as he clutched the end of the pew. "No," he said gently. "This is the *Banks* wedding — and it's *tomorrow,*" he added with subtle sarcasm.

"Surely," agreed the organist and disappeared through the gloom of the side aisle

By six-thirty Kay and all but four of the bridal party had appeared. The minister was still absent. The groom was still absent. The ushers and bridesmaids who had made the great sacrifice stood in small groups glaring at Mr. Banks with unconcealed hostility. It was evident that each and all had torn themselves away from agreeable situations for what they clearly considered to be an old-fashioned whim of Mr. Banks'. By their attitude they said, "You got us here. You ruined our fun. Now what are you going to do about it?"

It made Mr. Banks nervous. He distributed the seating lists to the ushers and made a little talk about over-all strategy. Somehow it didn't go very well. They listened to him with the detached boredom of tourists harangued by a Grand Canyon guide. Their aspirations were obviously elsewhere.

"I wonder where Mr. Galsworthy is?" asked Mr. Banks for the tenth time.

"Oh, he's somewhere. He's always late," said Mr. Tringle amiably. "I run the rehearsal."

"But some of the bridal party aren't here yet," protested Mr. Banks. "The groom isn't here. Nobody's here."

"Some of the bridal party is never here," said

Mr. Tringle. "The groom don't do nothing in weddings. Everything goes all right. You see. Don't worry. Now if you young ladies will line up in pairs outside that there door —"

They lined up, tittering and unwilling, as people line up for a group photograph which nobody wants taken. Once in place they unlined immediately. Mr. Tringle pushed them back like errant cattle. "O.K., Fritz," he yelled irreligiously. The organ suddenly gave a series of bumps and broke into the wedding march. Mrs. Banks watched nervously from a pew.

"It's too fast," she cried hopelessly as the skeleton procession dashed past her. "You're running. It's awful."

"You want to do it again?" asked Mr. Tringle, rubbing his hands with the air of one who has staged a great dramatic spectacle. "It comes O.K. next time. Take it easy. Line up now. Hey, you. Big girl. You get in back row this time so's they can see the other brides-maids. O.K., Fritz, shoot," he bawled.

They were off again. It wasn't the way Mr. Banks had pictured it. In fact, it reminded him more of the mob scene in the *Vagabond King* than a wedding rehearsal. He gave a sigh of relief as he saw the Reverend Galsworthy enter the church, trotting like a pony and exuding geniality. Now they would get the situation in hand.

"Well, well, well," said Mr. Galsworthy. "All over, I see. That means I'm just in time. So sorry. Had a meeting. Mr. Tringle's an old hand, though." He put his arm around Mr. Tringle's shoulder and squeezed him with impersonal affection. "Do they know their stuff, Mr. Tringle? Good. Well, I'm sure it will all go off very smoothly and that it will be a beautiful wedding."

Mr. Banks could hardly believe what he heard. "But they haven't really begun to rehearse. Four of the bridal party aren't even here yet and the groom isn't here either. They tried it a couple of times and it was awful."

Mr. Galsworthy looked at his watch and clucked.

"They do all right," said Mr. Tringle. "O.K. tomorrow."

"Good," said Mr. Galsworthy. "Good. I have a meeting now. As for the groom — well, the groom is not very important at weddings, is he, my dear?" He smiled benignly at the wispy bridesmaid under the impression that she was the bride-to-be.

"You're not nervous, are you, dear?" he continued, taking the wispy girl's hand in his. "No, of course not. Have your young man call me in the morning. I'll put him through his paces. I hate to rush, but I must. Don't worry. Everything will be fine."

Mr. Banks opened his mouth. "But —" A secretarial-looking person bustled down the aisle. "Mrs. Banks? There's a phone call for you in the Rector's office. I believe it's the groom's father and mother. They're at your house and they want to know if the rehearsal's over. I think the groom is with them."

"Sure," said Mr. Tringle cheerily. "Rehearsal's all over. Tell 'em to take it easy. Everybody'll be right home."

"Don't forget to have the groom call me in the morning," said Mr. Galsworthy. "Now don't worry. It will go beautifully tomorrow. I know. You see I've done this before."

"But —" began Mr. Banks. Then he looked around. The bridal party had disappeared, bearing Kay and the wispy girl with them. Mr. and Mrs. Banks shook hands cordially with Mr. Galsworthy and followed them.

On the way out Mr. Banks noted that most of Miss Bellamy's beautifully typed seating lists had been laid on the seats of pews and abandoned. He gathered them up. With the extras there might be enough for a redistribution.

"I do hope —" said Mrs. Banks.

"So do I," agreed her husband.

They went home to dress for the party at the Club.

Chapter 13

THEY'RE COMING INTO THE STRETCH

Mr. Banks awoke early the following morning, conscious that many things were wrong. The first to register positively was his body, which felt as if it had been run over. He moved his head on the pillow. For a moment he was convinced that his skull had been fractured.

Gradually he became aware that there was something particularly unusual about this day that was beginning so inauspiciously. Then his slowly awakening mind grasped the fact that he had come home rather late from the Country Club and that in a few hours his oldest child was going to be married.

Instinctively he turned to look out the window. The sun was shining. A cool breeze stirred the leaves of the maple tree outside. His eyes traveled lower and encountered those of the mother of the bride. They were appraising

145

him with an expression that struck him as being on the cold side.

"Nice day," he said.

"Yes," she said, "thank God. And now we're getting up. There's work to be done."

Mr. Banks would have given a year of life to lie quite still, indefinitely, but he felt the moment was a poor one for advancing whimsical ideas. As unostentatiously as possible he went to the bathroom cabinet and poured a large spoonful of Bromo Seltzer into a glass of water. It fizzed delightfully against his dry palate. The world looked better, although his sensations were still those of a sleeping leg. Perhaps this was a day when a bit of numbness might be helpful.

Downstairs the house was unrecognizable. The furniture had disappeared. The whole place smelled, not too faintly, of floor wax and soap suds. Delilah met him at the foot of the stairs.

"Mis' Banks, yo's goin' t'have yo' breakfas' in th' kitchen this mo'nin'," she announced. The idea seemed to strike her as high comedy. She disappeared into the pantry doubled up with laughter.

Mr. Banks ate his eggs self-consciously at Delilah's white-enameled table. It seemed to him that women used poor judgment about such matters. Why couldn't he have had his breakfast in the usual way and in the usual place? There was plenty of time to get things ready. No need for all this jitter.

After a second cup of black coffee he wandered aimlessly through the bare rooms. A truck pulled into the driveway followed by a black sedan from which a bald-headed man alighted. The front door was open. The bald-headed man walked in without ceremony. "I'm Tim's man," he said.

"Oh," said Mr. Banks, pleasantly, but with reserve.

"I guess we'll be settin' up th' flowers an' stuff," said Tim's man.

"Yes indeed," said Mr. Banks.

Mr. Tim's man stuck his head out the front door. "Lug 'em in, boys."

A few minutes later the floor of the living room was covered with potted plants, ferns and lumps of damp earth. Mr. Banks strolled restlessly through the debris and out the French door into the back garden. There he found three strangers unrolling a huge bundle of canvas.

"Is that the marquee?" he asked.

"It's the tent for the Banks weddin'," corrected one of the men.

Mr. Banks squinted at the cloudless sky. A brilliant idea flashed across his thrifty mind.

147

"You know," he said casually, "on a day like this I don't think we'll need a tent. I think it would be pleasanter to walk through that door right onto the open lawn. Don't you think so yourselves?"

The men stopped unrolling the tent and stared at him in silent amazement. One of them finally recovered his voice. "Don't need a tent!" he exclaimed. "Listen, Jack, this here tent is *con*tracted for three weeks ago. There's people yellin' for it all over th' place. You're just lucky, that's all."

"Yes, of course," said Mr. Banks. "I only thought – Yes, of course."

He stepped around the bulky pile and walked down the driveway. Maple Street was quiet. Several houses away his new neighbor, Mr. Hoggson, was cutting his front lawn. It seemed incredible to Mr. Banks that anyone could be engaged in such trivial work at a time like this. He strolled aimlessly toward him.

"Hi," said Mr. Hoggson, pausing. "Going to be a nice week-end."

"I certainly hope so," said Mr. Banks. "My daughter's getting married this afternoon."

"Well, you don't say so!" Mr. Hoggson relinquished his moist grip on the handles of the lawn mower and shook Mr. Banks' hand warmly. "That's your first child to go, isn't it?

148

Quite a wrench, all right. You bring 'em up to the best you got and spend a lot of money educatin' 'em an' then they run off with some football player an' that's the last you hear of 'em till you get a post card from Reno. Well, I certainly wish her all the happiness in the world. You won't come in and have a spot, perhaps? You got a hard day ahead of you."

"Sorry," said Mr. Banks. "We're kind of busy at the house this morning. I'm just doing an errand for my wife."

He walked briskly away without the slightest notion where he was going. It was the same everywhere. The world was proceeding quietly about its week-end tasks, heedless of what was happening at 24 Maple Drive. After about a mile he cut through a patch of woods and came back through the village in order to avoid Mr. Hoggson.

By the time he returned to the house the artisans had given way to relatives. The place was swarming with them. They had all made a great effort to be present. Now that they were here they wanted attention.

The phone was ringing continuously. He took charge of it. Anything was better than making conversation. The phone at least demanded concrete answers. Uncle Joe was in town and wanted detailed instructions on how to get out to Fairview Manor. Cousin Bertha was at the station. Would someone come down and get her? Aunt Harriet had lost her suitcase with her best dress in it. Would someone look around the house and see if she had left it there by any chance?

Mr. Banks said he would find it for her and tiptoed up the back stairs. But he was not looking for Aunt Harriet's suitcase. He was looking for Kay. He had suddenly noticed that she was not around.

Her door was closed. When there was no answer to his knock he opened it and looked in. Kay was lying on the bed, her face buried in the pillow, her shoulders shaking.

"Kitten," he said, "what's the trouble?"

She motioned him away violently, but he came over and sat on the side of her bed, running his fingers up and down her spine as he used to do when she was going to sleep.

"Tell me about it. What's hurt you? You shouldn't cry today, Kitten. This is your wedding day."

"Oh, I know it, Pops. That's just the *trouble*. It's my wedding day, but it *isn't*. It's everybody *else's* wedding day but it just isn't *mine.*" She let her face down into the pillow again, but now she was quieter.

Mr. Banks rubbed her back for a few

minutes without answering. "I know," he said finally. "I know. Mine either."

The Bill Harcourts gave a luncheon before the wedding. It was to have been a small affair: just the bride and groom, the bridal party and the immediate family. Nothing about this wedding, however, seemed capable of remaining small.

The house was crowded with people when Mr. and Mrs. Banks arrived. The bridesmaids, made confident by the conspicuous newness of their clothes, exuded vitality and youth. The ushers, on the other hand, had the drawn, haggard look of men who have just completed a dangerous bombing mission. They grabbed the cocktails from the passing trays as the occupants of a life raft would seize a wounded albatross as it floated by.

The place was alive with relatives whose names Mr. Banks could not remember. It was obvious that they were all out for a field day and expected him to meet their mood.

As he entered the room a barge of a woman, wearing pince-nez, bore down on him like a tugboat, backed him neatly between some bookcases and the piano and began a detailed account of Buckley's early childhood. She was up to his fifth year with nineteen years to go, and no sign of faltering, when someone spilled a plate of lobster salad on one of her ample hips. In the confusion Mr. Banks managed to escape, only to be recaptured by a man with a walrus mustache.

This character appeared to regard the gathering as a kind of public forum. He drew Mr. Banks to a window seat. This was the first opportunity he had had for a quiet chat, owing to the unaccountable confusion which seemed to pervade this whole affair. His primary interest was in world politics and his mind would not be at rest until he had Mr. Banks' opinion of the international situation. When Mr. Banks disclosed the fact that he had no opinions on the international or any other situation, the floor passed to the stranger, who obviously had a direct wire to God.

Athletic young men kept coming up with plates heaped to the gunwales with lobster and chicken salad, to which buttered rolls clung precariously. Mr. Banks felt slightly bilious and compromised on a cup of soup and a highball.

Kay approached them. "Mother's looking for you. She thinks we'd better be getting home." He gazed at her with awe. An hour ago she had been sobbing on her bed. Now she looked radiant — like a goddess of spring — serene and beautiful.

Mrs. Pulitzski, who had made over Mrs. Banks' wedding dress for Kay, had insisted on coming to the house that afternoon to be sure that all was in order.

"Good God," said Mr. Banks to the world at large, "this is a swell time to find out if it fits her. What's the woman going to do? Start making alterations now? Do you people realize it's a quarter to three and that there's a wedding in an hour and forty-five minutes?"

Any allusion to the passage of time always called forth a protest from Ben and Tommy.

"Gee, Pops, you might think it took us an hour to dress."

"Why, I can be dressed in ten minutes." Tommy stretched out languidly on his bed. "It won't take me ten minutes to get into that old fool suit."

Mr. Banks pushed down his temper with an effort. This was no time for a test of strength. "You two boys have a big responsibility this afternoon," he said with feigned calm. "You're the only two ushers who know our family. You're taking our car and you're to get there by four o'clock."

"We'll be there, Pops. Don't worry. Just relax."

Mr. Banks gave up and went to his room to dress. Somehow he felt alone and out of the

153

picture. Mrs. Banks was dressing in the guest room which adjoined Kay's. He made his preparations moodily.

He was not nervous, as he had feared he might be, only confused and ill at ease. While he regarded himself gloomily in the mirror Tommy burst into the room.

"Hey, Pops, I haven't anything but soft shirts. These stiff collars won't fit on soft shirts. What am I going to do?"

If Mr. Banks had had a blunt instrument in his hands he would undoubtedly have used it. As it was he merely stared at Tommy without affection.

"What size do you wear?"

"Fourteen and a half."

"Well, I wear fifteen and a half, so that's that. Hasn't Ben got a shirt without a collar?"

"Yeah, but he's got it on."

"Didn't you have an evening shirt?"

"Yeah. Mom put it in the wash. *Can't* I wear a soft shirt, Pops?"

"No," shouted Mr. Banks.

"Well, what'll I *do?*"

"Take the car and *get* one," yelled Mr. Banks. "Good God, it's quarter after three. You and Ben are due at the church in forty-five minutes. Have I got to think for —"

But Tommy was gone. Mr. Banks resumed

dressing, musing on the sordid eugenic tricks that Nature plays on men. When he had finished he surveyed himself in the long mirror and found the sight rather pleasing. Not many of his friends could wear their old cutaways at their daughters' weddings. If he didn't move impulsively it was perfect.

He started downstairs. As he passed Kay's door he heard voices. He was about to stop. Then the feeling of strangeness came over him once more and he continued on his way.

Without premeditation he found himself in the pantry. There he poured himself a highball which he regarded contemplatively for some time before drinking. When he had finished it he could think of nothing else to do so he started back upstairs.

Tommy almost knocked him down as he came leaping up the steps three at a time, a package under his arm. "I got it," he panted from the door of his bedroom. "I had to move some. A cop stopped me, but I talked him out of it. Gee, what a ride." His door slammed. Mr. Banks shuddered. He stood uncertainly at the head of the stairs, not knowing just where to go. A low murmur of voices came from behind Kay's closed door.

"Hi, Pops, this kind of a shirt has to have studs. Got any?" He felt himself going rigid again.

"You *must* have some. Your mother gave you a set for your evening shirt."

"I know, Pops. I can't find 'em. Must have gone to the wash."

In his bedroom Mr. Banks pawed vainly through the jewel case which had stood on his bureau for decades. It contained a miscellaneous collection of old fraternity pins, unidentified skeleton keys, a patent nail-clipper and his World War I identification tag. No collar buttons.

His voice sounded strained and unreal. "Listen, you've had two months to think of this. You take Ben to the church. Then go and get your damn collar buttons — and swallow them."

Tommy opened his mouth to protest at this injustice, but he saw an expression on his father's face that made him think better of it. He went out, closing the door quietly behind him.

A moment later Mrs. Banks entered the room and Mr. Banks forgot everything else. He knew that he would never be able to remember what she was wearing. He knew also that, to his dying day, he would never forget her as she stood, framed in the doorway, waiting for his approval — slim, graceful and lovely. All the beauty of her own wedding day

156

lay upon her, tempered by a serenity and dignity that made Mr. Banks feel suddenly shy.

She saw the startled admiration in his face. "Don't say any more, darling," she said. "You like it. I saw that. You'll spoil it if you try to tell me why. And for heaven's sake don't muss my hair."

"Kay is ready," announced Mrs. Pulitzski. They filed down the hall after her. She paused before Kay's door and threw it open dramatically. Kay was standing in the middle of the room, her train and veil carefully arranged behind her, no longer a brown-haired girl of five feet four, but a princess from some medieval court. Her head was thrown back slightly and she watched the effect upon her courtiers with the calm assurance of one born to the cloth of gold.

Mr. Banks would not have been surprised if she had extended her hand for him to kiss. His eyes became suddenly blurred. Good God, this would be a hell of a time to start crying. What was the matter with everybody today?

"You're wonderful, Kitten. Wonderful."

She squeezed his hand. "Thanks, Pops." For an instant her eyes met his — not as a daughter but as a woman. "Now, on to the slaughter," she said.

He looked at his watch. "Good God, it's five after four."

"The cars *must* be here," said Mrs. Banks. "I ordered both of them to be here at four sharp." She looked out Kay's window into the empty street.

"I'll call the garage," said Mr. Banks. "I'll give them a piece of my mind." Before he was halfway downstairs the telephone rang.

"Hello. – Yes. Speaking. – WHAT? WHO? Wait a minute." He covered the receiver with his hand. "It's those two cousins of yours from Baltimore. They came as a surprise. They're down at the station and there aren't any taxis. They want to know how they're going to get to the church."

Mrs. Banks stared blankly down at him over the stair rail.

"Well, what'll I tell them?" asked her husband. "They're *your* relatives."

"Tell them – tell them – Oh, tell them I don't give a damn how they get there. Tell them to jump in the lake and swim."

If Mrs. Banks had done a hand stand on the banisters she could not have startled her husband more. "Ellie can't be disturbed at the moment," he said apologetically to the telephone. "I'm sure there'll be a taxi along in a minute, though. There always is. – Yes indeed. It was good of you to come. – I certainly hope so."

The two black limousines drove up at quarter after four, their drivers immaculate in whipcord uniforms and visored caps.

"Where the hell –" began Mr. Banks.

The driver of the rear car got out and stood before Mr. Banks, cap in hand. He had white, wavy hair and a pontifical face that radiated gentle loving-kindness.

"I'm sorry, sir," he said. His voice sounded like a benediction. "They gave us the wrong address. I'm truly sorry, sir. I know the importance of punctuality at a time like this. I hope it hasn't upset the young lady."

Mr. Banks deflated visibly. "Not at all," he said. "Not at all." He helped Mrs. Banks and her mother into the front car, which dashed off immediately. Mrs. Pulitzski already had Kay carefully folded into the rear one. He climbed in beside his daughter, knocking his high hat over his nose. The white-haired chauffeur closed the door tenderly.

It was immediately opened again by a small man in a brown suit. "I'm Weisgold," he said. "Weisgold of Weisgold and Weisgold. The candid men." Mr. Banks' eyes shut as a blinding flash went off in his face. "Thanks," said

Mr. Weisgold. "See you in church."

"Drive," said Mr. Banks to the saintly wheelsman, "as if the seven hounds of hell were on your tail."

Chapter 14

WHO GIVETH THIS WOMAN?

Mr. Banks sat uneasily in the rear of the black limousine. Beside this lovely, calm stranger he felt small and a bit ridiculous. Their ages had somehow been mysteriously reversed. Instead of being the father of the bride he was a small boy being taken to dancing school in an asinine costume.

A neatly framed card on the back of the chauffeur's partition caught his eye. "The driver of this car is Mr. Pomus. He is Careful – Courteous – Co-operative." He read it over several times.

The shiny high hat cut his forehead. It had fitted him once. Why should it be too small for him now? He wondered if the forehead grew fat with the rest of the body. There was no reason why it should not, when you came to think of it. Or one's ears either, for that matter.

That was a quaint thought. "How stout your ears have grown, Mr. Banks."

Ruminating along these philosophical lines, he half observed their progress through the elm-shaded and self-consciously meandering streets of Fairview Manor. It should have created at least a ripple of disturbance. Someone should have stopped trimming a hedge long enough to step to the curb and wave them on their way. Someone should have cried, "There goes the bride and her father."

But no one did.

Solid citizens continued their ceaseless, neurotic fight to civilize nature with a pair of clippers and a lawn mower. Little boys continued their suicidal ball games under the very fenders of the car. In the front seat Mr. Pomus gazed benignly over his wheel. If he had raised two fingers in blessing to the urchins that he so nearly ran over, it would have been in character.

They rounded a corner into Red Brook Road. Far down its leafy vista Mr. Banks caught a glimpse of the striped awning in front of St. George's. Considerably nearer, however, was the father of all moving vans. A veritable freight car of a vehicle. It was backed against the curb and completely blocked the street. As they came to a stop the driver of this behemoth looked down on them from his cab with lack-luster eyes.

Mr. Pomus thrust his white locks through the window. "We want to get by," he said gently.

The driver eyed him impersonally as one observes passers-by in a station waiting room. "Hold yer glasses on, gran'pa. Don't let yerself get sweated up."

Mr. Pomus' face took on the ethereal look of a saint about to be martyred. "I'm telling you to pull that God-damn crate out of the way an' lemme get the hell by," he said with unexpected firmness.

The truck driver spat through the cab window as if to rid himself of an unpleasant taste. "Yeah? You an' who?"

Mr. Pomus opened the door quietly and half stood on the running board. From his lips there poured, without warning, a torrent of electric invective. It contained many words which Mr. Banks had not heard since World War I with adaptations of old ideas. For a few moments he stared at Mr. Pomus in dismay. Then something long dormant within him was touched into life.

Lowering the rear window and carefully removing his high hat, he stuck his head out and joined Mr. Pomus, adding a number of words that the latter seemed to have forgotten. For the first time that day he felt like himself. He also felt Kay tugging at his coattails.

The driver descended from his cab and approached them, his shoulders swaying like those of a boxer moving into the ring. When he reached the car he noticed Kay and stopped. "Whyn't you tell me you was on yer way to a weddin'? Jesus, what's bitin' people these days?"

He climbed back into his cab and stepped on the starter. Mr. Banks looked at his watch. It was twenty-three minutes past four. As they drew up to the curb in front of St. George's he noted the usual crowd grouped around the sidewalk openings of the striped awning. He alighted and, his hat once more knocked over his left eye, helped his daughter from the car.

She smiled up at him and took his arm. "You were wonderful, Pops." Mr. Weisgold of Weisgold and Weisgold danced before them like a leprechaun, his ever-candid camera at his eye. Preceded by flashing bulbs, they walked together toward the dim entrance of the church.

Mr. Tringle, radiating efficiency, was waiting for them at the top of the stone steps. "This way," he said, and dove into a small passage.

Through an open door Mr. Banks had a momentary glimpse of the interior of the church. He was conscious of heads and color and lights. It looked more like a stage backdrop than a real scene. The organ was booming complacently.

They were in some sort of vestibule that opened into the church through double doors that were now closed. The bridesmaids were there and a few of the ushers. Mr. Banks noted with surprise that everyone seemed dressed according to instructions.

Tommy appeared from somewhere, looking as if he were in the habit of wearing a cutaway and a wing collar every afternoon. "Sorry I messed things up, Pops," he said. "But I made it. Ben's going to take Mom down now."

Everyone seemed to know just what was going on except Mr. Banks. It was incredible that such complex details should be falling into place without his supervision. He almost resented it. With a dramatic flourish Mr. Tringle threw open the double doors that led into the church.

He saw Ben swing into the center aisle with his mother on his arm. A feeling of elation spread through Mr. Banks as he watched his wife's straight, slender back. For years she had been the focus of attention at all social events.

Now she was being led humbly to her place in a front pew. For once he had stolen the show.

The remaining ushers fell into line. Mr. Tringle stood beside the leaders. "Ready?" he asked. No one gave the slightest indication as to whether he was or not. Mr. Tringle pushed a small button on the wall.

The organ made a few ad lib sounds intended to convey the idea that the organist had come to the end of whatever it was he was playing. A hush fell over St. George's, broken only by the rustle of several hundred people trying to face in two directions at once.

This was the supreme moment – the moment Mr. Banks had dreaded and anticipated for so many weeks. It had all come with such a rush at the end that he scarcely had time to grasp its significance. Now that it was here, he was serenely calm. It was not an ordinary, workday calm, however, but rather one of detached unreality.

Although he had been in St. George's many times before it was as strange to him at this instant as a Byzantine mosque. The sea of faces that shot suddenly upward from the pews as the organ paused were unreal. They reminded him of a high-speed movie he had once seen of a growing poppy field. Even the girl beside him was a stranger. She was no longer his little

166

daughter, but a beautiful, serene woman into whom all wisdom had suddenly and mysteriously flowed. She stood, poised on the threshold of her greatest adventure, her face lit with understanding and confidence.

It was difficult to conceive how an earthly chap like Buckley could have produced this miracle. Having produced it, his responsibility to maintain it was great. It would be a terrible thing to betray that expression in Kay's eyes. They were fixed far beyond Buckley, on an ideal which perhaps no mortal could hope to achieve, but which was all the more precious because of its unattainability. A thousand generations of women were standing behind Kay now. For a mystic instant she was a generic part of that selfless, intuitive race which since the days of the mastodons has been quietly guiding awkward, bumbling Man to an unknown destiny of greatness.

At this particular instant he was horrified to note that two of the bridesmaids had begun to sniffle. In the unscrupulous way of all women in little things they had snatched carefully folded handkerchiefs from ushers' pockets and were dabbing their eyes and blowing their noses.

"Good God," said Mr. Banks, but he had not time to develop the idea. The organ sounded off with its warning thumps. Kay patted his arm. "Well, Pops, we're off."

"O.K. with the right foot," hissed Mr. Tringle. "*Right* foot, I said." Mr. Banks shifted quickly. Everyone else changed step at the same moment and he had to shift back again. Good God, was this a wedding march or a minuet? The procession passed through the oak doorway into the church.

Mr. Banks and Kay reached the rear pews. He would have continued, but she held him back. "Hold it, Pops," she murmured. With the calmness of a general watching his forces deploy into battle, she stood poised, awaiting the proper moment.

The maid of honor was twenty feet ahead when he felt the gentle pressure of her arm. The stage was set as she wished it. She was ready for her entrance.

Out of the corners of his eyes Mr. Banks caught glimpses of familiar faces. Their expression paid tribute to the girl at his side. Pride dispelled all other emotions.

He saw Buckley and the best man waiting for them at the end of the aisle. Mr. Galsworthy stood on the chancel steps smiling ever so slightly. Mr. Banks was struck by his resemblance to Mr. Pomus.

Now they were lined up before the steps and

the minister was reading from a white satin book with a purple marker hanging from it. As he stood on the top step he towered above them in his robes like a genie emerging from a bottle.

It gave Mr. Banks an entirely new view of Mr. Galsworthy's face — a kind of worm's-eye view. He became visibly aware of the minister's nostrils, which were unusually long and worked in and out like bellows as he spoke. He wrenched his eyes away with an effort, conscious that this was not the memory he wished to treasure in later years. At a moment like this it did seem as if he might be doing something more worth while than studying Mr. Galsworthy's nostrils.

Besides which he had a cue coming. When Mr. Galsworthy reached the place where he asked, "Who giveth this woman — ?" Mr. Banks was to say, "I do." It was his only line in the show. He wanted to acquit himself creditably and began to consider his delivery.

Should he say, *"I* do" or "I *do"*? *"I* do" sounded silly. It implied that any number of people might do it and that he was pushing himself forward for the job.

On the other hand "I *do"* didn't make much sense either. It certainly wasn't the proper way to answer a general question. The whole passage struck him as fatuous. It put the minister in a ridiculous position, forcing him to overlook the fact that the father of the bride was standing right under his nose – no! – not that! – not his nose again! – keep off that. But he was obliged to put the question in such a way that it carried the implication that perhaps *no one* would wish to undertake the job.

It all struck Mr. Banks as lacking in forthrightness. Obviously, however, this was an inappropriate time to suggest revision of the marriage service, so he decided on *"I do."* His next problem was the tone of voice to be used.

He didn't want to mumble it in a shamefaced kind of way. On the other hand if he boomed it out it would have an eager-beaver quality suggesting that he was delighted to get Kay off his hands. He compromised on a well-modulated, dignified delivery; about the tone a man would use if someone asked who would volunteer for a dangerous mission.

He was mindful of the fact that, when his one line had been spoken, his final part played, he was supposed to drop back a step, turn on his heel, and join his wife in the front pew. He wished that he had noticed just what lay in his immediate rear. He had an unpleasant vision of stepping back and tripping over something unexpected like an upturned corner of carpet or the end of the pew. He began to reach behind him stealthily with his right foot, using it like the antenna of an insect. He hoped that no one would notice it. People were always so quick to attribute such fumblings to alcohol.

"Who giveth this woman – ?" intoned the rich baritone of the Reverend Mr. Galsworthy from far above him.

It caught him off guard in spite of all precautions. Kay nudged him and placed her hand in his. "*I* do," he murmured almost inaudibly, and passed her hand to Buckley. As he performed the simple act he was conscious that something deep within him ripped slightly.

He did not see the rest. Turning slowly, he stared defiantly at the rows of faces, then entered the first pew and stood beside Mrs. Banks. He tried in vain to listen to the words of the service – and then suddenly it was all over.

It seemed impossible, but it was definitely over. Kay and Buckley were kissing. The organ had broken into the joyous notes of the Mendelssohn Wedding March, like a little boy released from Sunday school into spring sunshine. The maid of honor was struggling with Kay's train. The wedding guests were searching under the pews for lost gear and poking out hats that wives had sat on.

Kay beamed at them happily as she went by,

171

her arm through Buckley's, and again Mr. Banks felt that queer little rending in the center of his being. The flashing of bulbs indicated that Weisgold and Weisgold were still their old candid selves. Tommy appeared, to take his mother out.

It was over. The wedding dress, the bridesmaids' dresses, the struggles with cutaways, the invitations, the flowers, the lists, the rehearsal, the arguments, apprehensions, doubts and bewilderments had all suddenly become memories.

A wedding was like the experimental explosion of an atom bomb, thought Mr. Banks as he walked out behind his wife, smirking to right and left. You made the most careful preparations for months, then someone like Mr. Tringle pressed a button – and it was all over. There was scarcely any present tense in connection with weddings. They existed either in the future or in the past.

"Stanley, your hat looks like a cat in a thunderstorm," said Mrs. Banks as they descended the entrance steps of the church. "But it was lovely, darling, wasn't it?"

Chapter 15

RECEPTION

It is traditional that, between the church and the house, wedding guests are free agents. This is the one period in the schedule where they can express their own individuality.

The majority appreciate this unsupervised interlude and are apt to turn it into a kind of hare-and-hound race in which the bride, groom and immediate progenitors are the hares, the guests assuming the role of hounds.

The latter are held in check briefly by a few yards of satin ribbon and a rear guard of ushers whose hearts are no longer in their work. Scarcely have the hares disappeared down the striped tunnel of awning than the pack is after them with lolling tongues.

Gone the little pre-wedding courtesies when one car waited politely for another to pull in to the curb and friends exchanged genial words of greeting while trying to crawl out of under-slung sedans. Now it is every man for himself, *sauve qui peut,* and devil take the hindmost, for the last man to arrive at the house knows that he must spend the balance of the afternoon standing in the reception line watching his more active neighbors guzzling free champagne.

Mr. and Mrs. Banks arrived at 24 Maple Drive a few minutes behind the bridal party. During their absence Mr. Massoula had taken over completely in accordance with his promises. His Buckingham Caterers were darting about like Walt Disney gnomes.

Mr. Massoula met them at the front door. "Everything is in hand," he said. "Don't worry about anything. Go right into the living room. They're taking pictures of the bridal party."

In the living room Mr. Weisgold of Weisgold and Weisgold was perspiring freely and photographing the bridal party in various combinations. Those not engaged in being self-consciously photogenic stood about making wisecracks about those who were, between deep draughts of Mr. Banks' champagne, which had already begun to flow. A Buckingham representative approached with a tray full of glasses.

Mr. Banks took one. He felt like those men in the whiskey ads who go through nerve-

174

shattering experiences in jungles or on mountain precipices, then, their job well done, settle down calmly with friends in the last picture to a glass of their favorite grog. He had also gone through his own private ordeal and, he thought complacently, not without distinction. Now it was all over but the shouting. "Don't go away," he hissed to the waiter.

The bridesmaids were being photographed. Finally the Bankses and the Dunstans took their places before the flash bulbs. Mr. Weisgold's ability to produce an endless supply of bulbs fascinated Mr. Banks. The man must have been a hand grenade thrower in the war.

Over Mr. Weisgold's shoulder he suddenly noticed a cluster of faces in the doorway of the living room. Behind them were other faces. Faces jammed the front doorway. Through the window he could see them stretching in close formation halfway down the walk. Mr. Massoula blocked the entrance to the living room with firm urbanity, like the headwaiter of the Persian Room on a busy night.

The faces that peered at him were not of the happy, laughing type traditionally associated with wedding feasts. They were, rather, the glum, frustrated faces of those who had broken their fenders to get there early and were now denied the fruits of their sacrifices. They were the faces of citizens who definitely wanted to get this runkydunk over with and proceed with the main business of the afternoon.

Mr. Weisgold stopped flashing. The receiving line suddenly snapped to attention as if at the bark of a phantom drill sergeant. Mr. Massoula stepped aside nimbly to avoid being trampled. Mr. Banks never had a connected memory of the next forty-five minutes.

No one had told him whether or not he was to be part of the receiving line. For a moment he decided against it. Then it occurred to him that if he just stood in the middle of the living room he might be mistaken for the caterer. He slid quietly into place between his wife and Mrs. Dunstan as the first guest began to pump Mrs. Banks' arm.

It became immediately apparent that one of his duties was to introduce the guests to Mrs. Dunstan. Introducing one old friend to another had always been enough to give him complete aphasia. On ordinary occasions when guests arrived he disappeared into the pantry and busied himself with the refreshment department, leaving to Mrs. Banks the task of making people known to one another.

Those who were now so eagerly pushing forward to shake his hand were, for the most part, lifelong friends. In spite of this he fell

176

immediately into his accustomed groove and could not remember anyone's name. Occasionally he would recollect their first names, but he couldn't very well say to Mrs. Dunstan, "This is Joe and Booboo." For once his retreat to the pantry was blocked.

Mrs. Banks felt herself jabbed from the rear with a thumb. She jumped slightly and turned toward her husband with the injured look common to all people when jabbed unexpectedly from the rear. "Sing out the last names," he whispered desperately.

Mrs. Banks glanced at him anxiously. She knew he had been going through a considerable strain, but she had hoped with all her being that he would hold together for another couple of hours. "Why, Jack and Nancy *Hilliard,*" she cried gaily. "My dear, you look adorable. Yes. Wasn't it. I am so glad you thought so. And Grace *Lippincott,* I am so glad you could get here."

"Mr. and Mrs. Lippincott," mumbled Mr. Banks uncertainly in the general direction of Mrs. Dunstan. "I mean — that is to say — Mr. and Mrs. Hilliard."

He gave it up. He found that, by turning to the next pair of guests before they left Mrs. Banks, it was possible to pass up the whole business and let Mrs. Dunstan rock along as best she could. After all, she would probably never see any of these people again. Maybe she had something there.

Mr. Weisgold struggled through the line. "Look-it," he complained. "You told me you was goin' to have somebody with me to tell me who to shoot. I can't shoot no specials if I dunno who they are."

Mr. Banks looked despairingly around for Ben and Tommy. He had covered this point with the greatest care. Both had assured him that they would not leave Mr. Weisgold's side come hell or high water. Now they had disappeared. "Good God," he said. "Find one of the boys. Find one of the ushers. I've got my hands full here and besides I don't know who these people are any more than you do. Shoot anybody for all I care. Shoot them all. How do you do. So nice to see you. Wasn't it? Yes, she *is* a grand girl."

"O.K.," said Mr. Weisgold. "You'll get what you get. I ain't no mind reader."

A battle-ax of a woman was wringing his hand. "Buckley is my sweetheart," she was saying. "I have known him since he was a little boy." She released his hand to indicate how very tiny Buckley was. "He used to visit us at North Deering, you know. I expect he's told you all about me. I am Mrs. Butterton. Mrs.

178

Matilda Butterton. Buckley was a darling little —" Mr. Banks took her great hand in both of his and transferred it to Mrs. Dunstan.

If only people wouldn't stop and talk. There should be a law requiring them to pass silently in front of receiving lines the way they did before the biers of statesmen. They were still pouring in the front door. Glancing through the window, he could see the line extending beyond his field of vision. God knew where it ended. Had someone issued a general invitation by radio?

"Well, well, well." It was Joe Bludsoe and his diminutive wife. Joe was exuding goodfellowship and looking as if he might have apoplexy at any moment. "So you're on your way to joining the grandfather's club, eh? Well, well, well, I'm glad you lived through the wedding. God, you certainly looked awful when you came down that aisle. I said to Martha, 'Let me go out and drag him off the course. He's never going to make it.' You don't look so good now either. Still look green. When Mary was married —"

He continued to pump Mr. Banks' arm rhythmically. Mr. Banks transferred him to Mrs. Dunstan without causing him to miss a beat. "How do you do, Mrs. Karp," he said. "It was good of you to come. Oh, excuse me. Of course. Mrs. Park. Why, of course I knew it. Yes, we couldn't be happier about the whole thing."

It was over at last and not a minute too soon. If another person had injected himself into the living room the receiving line would have been squeezed into the fireplace.

Something was wrong, very wrong, with Mr. Massoula's "circulation." Theoretically the guests were supposed to slither off the end of the reception line, through a French door, and into the marquee where Mr. Massoula had set up his bar and buffet tables. It was all laid out like a pinball game.

The first few couples to come off the line, however, had chosen the French door in which to hold a long, eager conversation. Those who followed had merely rebounded from this obstacle back into the living room. The pinball idea still held, but it was not working according to plan.

Mr. Massoula's gnomes were so efficient that no one needed to go to the bar anyway. They slid like eels through the melee, mysteriously carrying trays full of champagne glasses where no amateur could have transported an uncorked bottle.

It seemed to Mr. Banks that these busy little figures must be paid on a piece basis – so much per glass dispensed. Never had he seen men more devoted to their work. The moment a person tilted his glass they were at his elbow waiting eagerly with a fresh supply. It was true that he had told Mr. Massoula to keep things moving. He had merely been thinking of other weddings where he had stood around for hours with an empty glass talking to someone whose name he did not know. It was one thing to avoid that and another to hurl the stuff down people's throats every time they opened their mouths.

The sickening idea occurred to him that at this rate it would be all gone in half an hour. For the third time that day he felt damp and clammy. His emotions were beginning to set up a distasteful system of hot and cold running perspiration.

He decided to go to the marquee and investigate. As he started for the door he tripped over a dog which, he noted, was being followed by another dog. To the best of his knowledge he had never seen either animal before. However, even if they had been his two favorite canines this did not seem a proper place for dogs.

A lovely young creature approached.

"*Mr.* Banks," she cried. "What a darling, *darling* wedding. Kay looked too, *too* beautiful. You should be so *proud*, Mr. Banks. And Buckley's just *divine*. We are all crazy for him.

And Mrs. Banks looked too, too —"

"Where the hell are all the dogs coming from?" interrupted Mr. Banks. He had just noted a brown and tan number entering the room through the legs grouped in the French door. It was apparently in search of some friend. "Is this a Bide-a-Wee Home or a wedding?" He wondered if the Buckingham Caterers were beginning to pour his champagne into the neighborhood crossbreeds.

His unknown companion gave a silvery laugh. "Oh, Mr. Banks, that's *cute*. The place does seem to be getting filled up with pooches, doesn't it."

"Listen," said Mr. Banks. "Do me a favor. Get hold of Tommy or Ben, if they haven't left town, and tell them that part of an usher's job is to throw out livestock."

"Oh, I will, Mr. Banks. I will. That's darling." She gave him a look that might have meant anything — but didn't — and disappeared into the crowd. He made another start for the marquee, but the impromptu reunion in the French door had grown to such proportions that he gave it up for the moment and pushed his way about the room at random.

Later he could remember a roar of voices — and people making faces at him — and making faces back at people — but it was a scene which would remain forever out of focus in his memory. Eventually he felt a tug at his sleeve. Kay and Buckley were standing behind him, Kay holding her crumpled train over her arm and grinning.

"Hi, Pops. We're going to get ready now. Don't you want to see me hurl my bridal bouquet?"

He followed them to the front hall while the wedding guests whooped noisily after. Kay and Buckley were already looking down from the landing.

Mr. Banks was astonished to discover an entirely new expression on Kay's face. Vanished the ethereal look she had worn as they started down the aisle. Now her ordinarily placid features radiated a self-confident, roguish gaiety that he had never seen before.

For twenty-four years Kay had been as satisfactory a daughter as any man could desire. His only complaint, if one could use so strong a word, was that she was too repressed, too shy — not a scared rabbit exactly, but lacking that bold grasp of the realities which he admired in women.

He had thought of her thus handicapped, leaving the cloisters and facing the world, in all the intimacy of married life and with a man whom she scarcely knew. Until this moment it had seemed to Mr. Banks that convention forced a transition that was brutal in its suddenness and completeness – a transition floodlighted by a glare of publicity which convention also demanded. From Mr. Banks' point of view it was enough to make the boldest maiden hesitate.

Yet here was Kay, who only a few days before had been telling him that she didn't have the nerve to go through with it, standing beside Buckley on the landing, looking over the faces below her with all the happy, relaxed assurance of a hunting dog which has just retrieved a bird.

His eyes rested balefully for a moment on Buckley. Ordinarily a shy fellow in crowds, he now had a look of smug possessiveness that sent an unexpected wave of irritation down Mr. Banks' spine.

The maid of honor was jockeying for position under the landing. Kay was waiting for her with the bridal bouquet poised. Small chance for the eager virgins clamoring with outstretched arms, their faces expressing in half-light what glowed so brightly and unashamed in Kay's. It struck Mr. Banks that the accepted belief that men married women was a colossal hoax – they were merely married *by* women.

There was a shrill yelping as the bridal bouquet came sailing over the rail and fell, with its usual precision, into the outstretched arms of the maid of honor. Then Kay and Buckley disappeared around the corner of the stairs followed by the bridal party.

The crowd began to spread out again and Mr. Massoula's walking dispensaries, apparently refreshed by the pause, went into action with renewed enthusiasm. Again Mr. Banks was struck by the need for taking inventory and he turned once more toward the marquee. Ralph Dixon collared him at the French door. He was a lawyer who took two things in life seriously. One was Ralph Dixon, the other the law.

"Hello, Banks," he said.

Mr. Banks wished Ralph Dixon wouldn't call him "Banks." He considered himself equally successful as a lawyer and they were the same age. He realized that the English all addressed one another this way, but he wasn't English and when addressed as "Banks" he always felt like a stage butler.

He should, of course, have said, "Hello, Dixon." Instead he said, "Hi, Ralph."

"Nice wedding," said Mr. Dixon and apparently considered that he had thereby paid his tribute to the amenities. "Got a minute?"

185

"Well, the fact is —" began Mr. Banks with a sinking heart.

"It's about that Shatton matter," said Mr. Dixon. "I don't like to be on the other side of the fence from you, Banks, and I think in this case you're all wet. Now just take the facts."

Mr. Dixon then took the facts and laid them out in orderly rows for Mr. Banks' appraisal. A waiter appeared with champagne and as Mr. Banks drank it he suddenly realized that he did not have the slightest idea what Ralph Dixon was talking about. Perhaps this stuff was getting him. He decided to hold his glass quietly and not touch it for a few minutes.

It was all the same to Mr. Dixon, however, whether Mr. Banks understood him or not. He was marshaling his facts and he would have marshaled them with equal gusto if Mr. Banks had been stretched out insensible on a window seat.

"Heidee-ho, heidee-ho. This *is* a party." A pasty-faced gentleman with jowls like a bloodhound injected himself into the summation. It was Uncle Peter, who had come all the way from Sioux City and was obviously not going back empty. Although Mr. Banks had always privately considered Uncle Peter an old bum, at the moment he was delighted to see him.

"Peter," he said. "I want you to meet a friend

186

of mine, Mr. Dixon. Ralph, this is Peter Quackenbush — he's related to my wife," he explained parenthetically.

Mr. Dixon glared silently at Uncle Peter and gave evidence of being about to move away. This would have been merely a transference of evils for Mr. Banks. Danger made him alert. Within the bat of an eye he had disappeared through the French door.

Judging by the crowd in the living room he had expected to find the marquee half empty. On the contrary, it was also jammed with people. The temperature was midway between that of a Turkish bath and a greenhouse.

Mrs. Banks had hired a push-and-pull man to circulate among the guests. Mr. Banks discovered him standing unnoted by one of the tent poles, dressed in his interpretation of a Neapolitan costume, obviously bursting his lungs and his instrument in the public weal. The din in the tent was so great, however, that he might have been squeezing a blacksmith's bellows and gargling his throat. Mr. Banks wondered why, from an economic viewpoint if no other, his wife had considered it necessary to pay someone to add to a confusion which was contributed gratis.

In spite of the Buckingham boys, who were getting rid of Mr. Banks' champagne just as eagerly here as in the house, there was a crowd of eager customers in front of the bar table. He shouldered his way in and tried to get the attention of one of the sweating men behind it. They were engrossed in snatching bottles from huge tubs of icewater, uncorking them and dividing their contents between the massed glasses and the tablecloth.

A strange man next to Mr. Banks watched them with the tense concentration of a bird dog. "Lousy service," he said finally to Mr. Banks in what was obviously meant as a friendly opening.

"Terrible," agreed Mr. Banks.

"About on a par with the champagne," said the stranger.

"I thought the champagne was pretty good," said Mr. Banks defensively. "For American champagne, of course."

"Bilge," said the genial stranger. "Sparkling bilge. I regard all champagne as bilge, but some comes from a lower part of the hold than others. This comes from just over the keel." The young man took two dripping glasses and backed away.

Mr. Banks beckoned to one of the barmen.

"How is the champagne holding out?" he asked.

The barman looked at him coldly. "O.K.,

O.K.," he said. "Don't worry, mister. You'll get plenty." Mr. Banks found himself blushing, then he remembered the old Chinese proverb and decided to relax and have a look at the garden. It would be interesting to find out if it were also filled with people.

His progress through the tent was slow. Near the entrance he spotted Miss Bellamy talking to a group from the office. She detached herself and came toward him balancing a glass of champagne without too great success. He had never seen Miss Bellamy dressed like this before and it rather startled him. He didn't know just what to say, but she was obviously quite at ease.

"Boss, we certainly put on a wonderful wedding. Yes, sir. If I do say so, it was beautiful. I want to drink a toast. I want to drink a couple of toasts. First, to the bride. Say, you were swell coming down the aisle. No one would ever have known you were scared."

"Thank you," said Mr. Banks. Somehow or other this was not the self-effacing Miss Bellamy he had left at the office yesterday afternoon. They drank solemnly.

"And now I want to drink to the best boss in the world. Yes, sir, the finest boss in the world." She had certainly never looked at him quite like that before.

189

"And I'll drink to the finest secretary," said Mr. Banks, embarrassed.

"Oh, you're just saying that," said Miss Bellamy, her large brown eyes searching his face intently. "You're just making that up, I know you are. Got a cigarette?" As he lit her cigarette he wondered if the world could ever again be forced back into its comfortable old normalcy.

"You got to watch this stuff," said Miss Bellamy, gazing thoughtfully into her glass. "You got to watch it every minute. If you don't – it'll get you. No question about it. Want to know something?" She leaned toward Mr. Banks' ear. "That Miss Didrickson's plastered. She's the new one with the dyed hair. Come on over. The bunch will want to see you. She's a silly ass, though. I didn't like her from the start. She was saying –"

A young man in a cutaway approached. "Mrs. Banks is looking for you, sir. She sounds as if she wants to see you right away."

Relieved to have some objective, Mr. Banks began to fight his way back to the house. He had almost made the exit from the marquee when an enormous woman blocked his way. She was accompanied by a gangling young girl with a mouthful of braces.

"Oh, Mr. Banks, it was such a heavenly

wedding. I want you to meet my daughter Betsy. This is Kay's father, dear." Betsy tittered as if she found the idea grotesque. "Humphrey couldn't come." Mr. Banks cast vainly about in his mind for anyone by the name of Humphrey. "He wanted me to tell you how sorry he was. You were *so* nice to ask us. I said to Humphrey, 'That was *so* nice of the Bankses to include us. And to the reception too.' I brought Betsy. I didn't think you'd mind. She adores Kay so and she's been so excited about the wedding. Haven't you, dear?"

Betsy's excitement seemed to have died down since the ceremony. At the moment she looked like a captured German prisoner brought to headquarters for questioning. "Kay looked perfectly beautiful," continued the large woman. "Simply ravishing. And the brides-maids' dresses − Well, my dear, they were out of another world. I think the whole thing −"

A second young man in a cutaway approached. "Mrs. Banks is sort of tearing her hair out, sir. She said for me to tell you that Kay and Buckley are getting ready to go and where are you."

Mr. Banks made a mumbling noise and forced a passage between the stout woman and Betsy. Mrs. Banks pushed toward him through the crowded room. "Stanley Banks, where have you been? I'm almost crazy. I suppose you've been in that tent telling stories. Now come. Kay and Buckley will be coming down any minute."

Again there was a dense crowd in the front of the house. Mr. Massoula's henchmen moved through it bearing salad bowls filled with confetti. At least they were distributing something inexpensive for the moment. People were self-consciously grabbing handfuls, most of which they immediately let slip through their fingers to the floor. Everyone was watching the stairs tensely as if they expected a couple of whippets to come streaking down and out the door before they could get rid of the balls of damp paper in their clenched fists.

This was the scene that Mr. Banks had visualized so often during the last twenty-five years; the moment when his first-born would come running down a broad staircase on the arm of a muscle-bound stranger, to disappear from his life forever — at least in the role of his little daughter.

When he had stood at the foot of other people's staircases waiting to throw damp paper at their daughters, his heart had been warm with sympathy for the fathers of the brides, who strolled with such brave nonchalance among their guests. He had hoped that he would have equal courage when his time came.

Now that it was here he only felt numbness. He had rehearsed it all so often in his mind — he had hugged his private sadness to his bosom so many times — that its fulfillment was less real than its anticipation.

A bridesmaid peered around the corner of the stair landing, grinned sheepishly and disappeared. Someone cried, "Here they come," as if it were a horse race. Then Kay and Buckley, conspicuously new in every detail, were tearing across the landing and down the final flight of stairs with that hunched, headlong look of charging moose that Mr. Banks had observed in all brides and grooms coming downstairs.

They were on the front walk now, their shoulders covered with confetti, their heads still lowered between their shoulders. Mr. Banks was right behind them, running in form, the ushers and bridesmaids bringing up the rear in full cry. Buckley's car stood at the end of the walk. It was amazing how these details fell into place against all odds. They were in. Kay leaned through the open window while Buckley fought off ushers on the other side.

"Good-by, Pops. You've been wonderful. I love you."

The car lurched forward. Mr. Banks revolved off the rear mudguard into the arms of a bridesmaid. "Good-by, good luck." They were already half a block away. A few ushers, who had gone through the usual routine of almost being run over in the getaway, were brushing the dirt from their trousers.

When Mr. Banks returned to the house he realized that the reception had entered a new and final phase. Its connection with the bride and groom had already been forgotten. For all practical purposes the bride and groom themselves had been forgotten. The Reception had become a Party and only a few cutaways and bridesmaids' dresses recalled the event that had brought it into being.

The more conservative element began to leave. A few said good-by. The majority took advantage of the confusion and merely walked away. Officer Mullins, who had undertaken to act as parking attendant, had long since left his post and retired to the kitchen, where one or two other members of the force were already at work on material furnished by the ever-thoughtful Mr. Massoula.

Officer Mullins had packed the parking field efficiently and solidly before he left. This had been quite satisfactory during the parking, but unfortunately the guests were not departing on the modern accounting basis of last in first out. If there were any order to their leaving, it appeared to be just the opposite.

And so it came about that, while Officer Mullins exchanged views on wine and women with his fellow craftsmen, the more prominent citizens of Fairview Manor locked bumpers and cursed in the scarred field behind the house.

Mr. Banks felt restless. A sudden desire seized him to speed his parting guests. He wandered out of the house and across the lawn in the direction of the parking field, carefully balancing a glass of champagne as he walked. The scene which burst upon him as he rounded the lilac hedge reminded him of a picture in an old geography of sampans milling on a Chinese river front.

For the next half hour, disregarding the dangerous snugness of his cutaway, he leaped up and down on entwined bumpers, directed backing cars into other backing cars and helped angry citizens to pull their bashed mudguards free from their tires.

Then, retrieving his glass, which he had left on a fence post, he returned to the house, dirty but satisfied, feeling that for the first time in many hours he had been of some practical use in the world.

The bitter-enders were in full swing. The Neapolitan push-and-pull artist was hard and soundlessly at work in the living room, which was jammed with people, all of them obviously prepared to see the thing through to the final bottle.

Chapter 16

ALL OVER

The last guest had gone. The last damp hand had been wrung. The bridal party had disappeared noisily to seek bigger and newer adventure. The Dunstans had left. The relatives had returned to the oblivion from which they had emerged. Mr. and Mrs. Banks were alone with the wreckage.

They sat limply in two armchairs which Mr. Banks had dragged down from upstairs. The rug was covered with confetti. The few casual tables which Mr. Massoula had left in the living room were garnished with gray rings. Here and there on the white paint of the sills were the dark signatures of cigarettes. The floral background of the reception line obliterated the fireplace. They stared at it in silence.

"She did look lovely in that going-away suit," said Mrs. Banks dreamily. "Didn't you think it was good-looking?"

Mr. Banks couldn't remember it very well.

He knew she had had on something tan. There his detail stopped. But her face was etched forever on his memory as she stood on the landing waiting to throw the bride's bouquet.

"She's a darling," he said.

"Queer the Griswolds didn't come," mused Mrs. Banks. "They accepted and Jane told me they were coming."

"I don't see how you know whether they came or not."

"I know everybody that was here and everybody that wasn't," said Mrs. Banks complacently.

Mr. Banks did not question it. This woman who couldn't remember the details of the most elementary problem for five minutes would remember now and forever everyone who came, everyone who didn't – and also those who crashed the gate.

"My God," exclaimed Mrs. Banks, pressing her hand over her face. "We forgot to ask the Storers."

"We couldn't have," said Mr. Banks.

"We did, though."

"That's terrible. Couldn't we pretend we sent them an invitation? You could call Esther tomorrow and ask her why she didn't come."

"I might at that," said Mrs. Banks.

There was a brief silence. "What are we

going to do with all those presents?" asked Mr. Banks.

"I don't know. Somebody's got to pack them, I suppose. I think I'll just leave them as they are for a while."

"I guess that's the best thing," said Mr. Banks.

They lapsed into exhausted silence. In the brain of each a projector was unreeling the film of the day's events. It would have amazed them if they could have known how different the films were.

In another compartment of Mr. Banks' brain an adding machine was relentlessly at work. The figures came pouring out and each time they were greater than before.

"Didn't the decorations in the church look too lovely?" asked Mrs. Banks.

Mr. Banks was startled to discover that he had not even noticed if there were any decorations in the church. It was a relief to know that someone had checked on that dog-robber Tim.

"They were beautiful," he said simply.

"Mr. Tim did a wonderful job considering how little money we gave him to work with," said Mrs. Banks. Her husband started, then pressed his lips together and made no comment.

"I suppose," said Mrs. Banks, "we ought to

get out the vacuum cleaner and not leave this whole mess for Delilah tomorrow. I'll go up and change my dress."

Mr. Banks followed her upstairs glumly. Like a fog blowing in from the sea, he could feel the first wisps of depression fingering into his soul.

Here was the place where she had stood. He paused and looked over the rail at the confetti-strewn hall. Queer about places and houses. They remained the same yet they were never the same. By no stretch of the imagination was this the spot from which Kay had tossed her flowers to the waving arms below.

He continued up the stairs, thinking of all the money and energy that was wasted each year visiting the scenes of great events under the impression that they were still the same places.

At the door of the spare room where the presents were on display, he paused, then lit the light and went in. This morning it had been a gay, exciting place, full of anticipation and promise of things to come. The animating spirit was gone. Now it was just a bare room with card tables along the walls covered with china and glassware. It was as impersonal as a store.

He tried to shake off the cloud that was

settling over him. In the bathroom a single bottle of champagne rested quietly in the wash-basin. It had been put there by someone just before Mr. Massoula ran out. Heaven knew what for. It was still cold. For a moment he debated whether to open it. Then he turned, went downstairs and got out the vacuum cleaner.

An hour later the last particle of confetti had been transferred to the bulging bag of the machine. They sat once more in their chairs in the living room gazing with exhausted faces at the banked greens in front of the fireplace.

On the floor near the edge of the rug Mr. Banks spied a few bits of confetti that the cleaner had overlooked. He rose to pick them up. There seemed to be more just under the edge. He turned back the corner and disclosed a solid mat of multicolored paper.

Without comment he dropped the rug back into place. Mrs. Banks was watching, but said nothing. He went quietly up to the bathroom and drew the cork in the last remaining bottle. From the spare room he selected two of Kay's new champagne glasses and returned to his wife.

Carefully he filled the two glasses and handed one to Mrs. Banks. Behind the floral background the clock on the mantel struck twelve. The whistle of a train from the city hooted in the distance as it rounded the curve into the Fairview Manor station. A dog was barking somewhere.

"How," said Mr. Banks raising his glass.

"How," said Mrs. Banks.